A
Harlequin
Romance

OTHER
Harlequin Romances
by ROBERTA LEIGH

Many of these titles are available at your local bookseller,
or through the Harlequin Reader Service.

For a free catalogue listing all available Harlequin Romances,
send your name and address to:

HARLEQUIN READER SERVICE,
M.P.O. Box 707, Niagara Falls, N.Y. 14302
Canadian address: Stratford, Ontario, Canada.

or use order coupon at back of book.

CINDERELLA
IN MINK

by

ROBERTA LEIGH

HARLEQUIN BOOKS   TORONTO
WINNIPEG

Original hard cover edition published in 1973
by Mills & Boon Limited.

© Scribe Associates 1973

SBN 373-01783-9

Harlequin edition published May 1974

Printed in Canada

CHAPTER ONE

The slim, fine-boned girl running through the wraithlike tendrils of fog looked like a wraith herself, so delicate were her features, so gossamer-fine the wispy tatters of gauze that clung to her slim waist and swayed round her shapely legs. Even when she paused to make sure she was not being followed her skirts continued to sigh around her, gently moved by a grey mist that was fast thickening into fog. But there were no echoing steps to catch her attention and perceptibly she relaxed, lifting up her ragged skirts to let the material play through her fingers.

Something furry touched her legs and she gave a scream and jumped back, feeling foolish as she realised it was the mink wrap she was holding. Thank goodness she had had the sense to collect it from the cloakroom before running out of the house. Wrapping the fur around her, she buried her chin in its warmth, unaware of how incongruous it looked above the ragged dress.

Cinderella in mink. She had considered it amusing to go to Deborah Main's fancy dress party dressed like that. Jeffrey had thought so too, not only because it struck him as ironic that Nicola Rosten — heiress to a cereal fortune — should pretend to be Cinderella for a night, but because it enabled him to accompany her as Prince Charming, in an elegant costume that suited his tall blond looks.

'Why not use the party to announce our wedding date?' he had suggested. "It's ridiculous to have a long engagement."

"I've only known you two months," she reminded him. "And Marty thinks we should wait a bit."

"Your godfather would like nothing better than to have you an old maid," Jeffrey said sulkily. "That way he'd control your affairs for ever."

"I get control of everything when I'm thirty – married or not," she corrected him.

"You'd control it now, if you married me. That's why he dislikes me so much."

"He doesn't dislike you at all," Nicola lied, for though George Martin had never said anything against her fiancé, his excessively polite attitude towards him was sufficiently indicative of his feelings.

Not until a few nights ago, when she had finally tackled him about it, had he admitted his doubts about Jeffrey's suitability.

"In my day a man made sure he was in a good financial position before he thought of marriage; and Simonds is just beginning his career as a stockbroker."

"He has excellent prospects," she had said defensively.

"You can't live on prospects. If you were an ordinary girl, how would he have proposed to keep you?"

"He probably wouldn't have asked me to marry him." Seeing the look of triumph on George Martin's face, Nicola had sighed with exasperation. "Honestly, Marty, it would be childish for Jeffrey to pretend I was like any other girl. I mean, I haven't been since I was born, have I?"

"No." Her godfather had looked rueful, thinking of the Rosten millions that now increased on their own momentum. "Perhaps that was why I was hoping you'd meet someone who would treat you as if you *were* ordinary. It would do you good."

"It might do me good," she had laughed, "but I doubt if I'd like it?"

"How would you know? You've never had the experience."

"Nor likely to. Be a realist, Marty. I've as much chance of getting away from my heritage as a tortoise its shell!"

"You could at least be more particular about whom you invite to share your shell! Jeffrey's the third young man you've got yourself engaged to in less than a year."

"The other two didn't count. They were fortune-hunters!"

"And Simonds isn't?"

"He likes money," she had admitted. "Who doesn't? But he isn't in love with me because of it. After all, he comes from a good family and he's got money of his own. But it's *me* he loves, not the Rosten fortune."

"Are you sure?"

"As sure as I'll ever be," she had replied. "So promise to stop treating him like a leper."

George Martin had done his best to comply, going out of his way the next time Jeffrey came to the house, to take him to the library for a quiet man-to-man chat and a subsequent game of snooker. It was her godfather's unexpected friendliness towards him that had emboldened him to suggest she set the date for their wedding.

Yet she had refused. Looking back on it now, she found it hard to know exactly why she had done so. Instinct, perhaps. Yet honestly compelled her to admit it had been no such thing; merely a fear of tying herself down to another human being.

"We'll get married in the spring," she had hedged. "But there's no need to announce it. We'll decide on a date by ourselves, and elope."

"Suits me." He had pulled her into his arms and kissed her with an expertise that roused her to a response. But then Jeffrey was expert in everything he did, be it winning clients, charming old ladies or making love.

Tears filled her eyes and trickled down her cheeks, smudg-

7

ing her waterproof mascara so that little blobs of black marked her cheeks. It was hard to know which hurt the most; the knowledge that her godfather had been right about Jeffrey or that her own assessment had been proved so wrong. Either way the outcome was the same. By his own actions Jeffrey had closed the door on any future they might have had together.

Closed the door. The irony of the remark brought a bitter smile to her lips. If only she had *left* the door closed, had not barged into the library in search of her missing fiancé and promptly plunged the room into blinding light, causing two pairs of eyes to blink at her with guilt and two startled voices to flounder through feeble excuses.

"It meant nothing," Jeffrey had said, coming after her as she ran to collect her wrap. "You know what Deborah's like."

"So does everyone else!"

"It was only a kiss," he had said sulkily.

"Only?" she had flared, and remembering the loosened bodice and the pale curve of breast, had wrenched open the front door and plunged into the darkness.

At first she had heard Jeffrey racing after her, but running down one side street and then another she had soon lost him. Lost herself too, for looking around her at the tall houses barely visible through the fog, she had no idea where she was.

The mournful hoot of a ship's siren made her turn in the direction of the sound. If she could reach the Embankment she would at least have some idea of her bearings. Hurriedly she sped on, keeping close to the railings to give her a guideline. If anything the fog had grown thicker in the last few minutes. Or was it longer since she had run from the house? It was difficult to gauge time when your mind was in a state of chaos. Marty had been right after all – the way he always was about the young men she met.

"Fortune-hunters, the lot of them," he had once said.

Well, she wouldn't give him the chance to say it again. She was finished with men; finished with the hope of trying to find one who would love her for what she was and not what she possessed. Yet she had been so sure of Jeffrey. Remembering his ardent lovemaking she was nauseated with shame. All she had meant to him was an Aladdin's cave of blue-chip shares and Triple A property!

Her tears were falling faster, blurring a scene that was already blurred with mist. The hooter mourned again, louder this time, and she knew the river was close. The air certainly seemed damper and the mist lay heavy across her bare arms and long dark hair. Again the hooter sounded and this time as it died away she heard the throaty chug of a taxi.

Headlamps fought a path through the foggy white blanket, and she ran to the edge of the pavement and waved her arms. There was no change in the tempo of the engine and she realised that in a dark dress and fur she had no hope of being seen. But she had to stop the taxi. Heaven knew when she'd find another one.

"Taxi!" she cried, and darted into the road.

A small car, hugging the kerb as it came round the corner, caught her on the side of her thigh and sent her flying to the ground. The taxi chugged away into the fog, but the little car drew to a stop. A door opened and quick steps came towards her.

"I didn't see you," a frantic female voice said. "I wasn't doing more than ten miles an hour, but I didn't see you!" Hands bent to lift her, surprisingly strong hands when taken in conjunction with the quavery voice. "Are you hurt?"

"I don't think so," Nichola gasped, and felt herself shaking with reaction. "You should have had your headlights on. No wonder I didn't see you!"

"It makes the fog worse if you drive with headlamps on," the voice explained. "That's why I turned them off. I can see better without them."

"You didn't see *me*."

"I know, my dear, and I can't tell you how sorry I am." The woman pulled Nicola towards the car. "Do come in from the cold."

Nicola obeyed, and as she clambered into the seat a stabbing pain in her leg made her gasp.

"You *are* hurt," the woman exclaimed. "Give me your address and I'll take you home."

The word reminded Nicola of Jeffrey. That was where he would be: at home waiting for her; in the drawing-room, his handsome face full of contrition, his voice beseeching as he begged her to forgive him. And in the mood she was in at the moment – overwrought and shaken with pain – she was more than likely to do so.

"I can't go home," she said. "I can't!"

"Why not? Do you live far from here?"

"No. But I can't go home yet. Not like this."

There was a movement and a dim light suddenly illuminated the interior and the plain features of a middle-aged woman in a tweed coat. Myopic eyes behind gold-rimmed glasses stared at Nicola in consternation. "Oh, my dear," she said, "I hadn't realised. No wonder you don't want to go home. Have you had a very bad time?"

"Bad time?" Nicola echoed.

"Of course you have. Don't bother answering, my dear, it's quite obvious from the way you look." She touched Nicola's ragged dress and glanced at the bedraggled fur – wet from the muddy road – that still partially covered the bare shoulders. "I'd better take you to the Centre. I'm sure they'll be able to help you."

"I don't need help," Nicola said faintly, and closed her eyes. "If I could just rest a moment."

"You need to rest for the night," came the reply. "You're suffering from reaction; just sit quiet and leave everything to me."

The car throbbed beneath her and Nicola tried to sit up, but the quick movement made her feel dizzy and she closed her eyes again. It was warm and muggy inside the car, with a comforting smell of wet tweed and dog that reminded her of the school holidays she used to spend at Marty's house in Wales. How carefree she had been then; unaware of what it meant to be one of the richest girls in the world.

"Here we are," the woman said, stopping the car with a jerk. "Do you think you can manage to walk or shall I get someone to help you?"

"I can manage." Nicola gingerly clambered out and tottered into a hall. A wave of nausea gripped her, bringing a film of sweat to her face so that her skin glowed pale in the harsh white light beating down on her. "Where am I?" she whispered.

"At the Centre. You'll be quite safe here."

"Whose centre?" Nicola asked painfully, wishing that the bulb on the ceiling would stop swaying from side to side.

"Mine," a deep male voice said.

The tweedy woman gave a cry of pleasure. "Oh, Barnaby, I'm so glad you're here. I knocked this poor child over and –"

Nicola heard no more. Once again she felt she was falling, but this time strong hands caught hold of her and as she sank into unconsciousness she felt herself being cradled like a child.

"You've found a real Cinderella," the deep voice said. "But I doubt if this poor kid's ever had a fairy godmother."

CHAPTER TWO

Nicola opened her eyes and stared up into the glow of an orange-shaded bulb. She shifted her head and became aware of a lumpy pillow underneath her and a rough grey blanket over her body. Her brows drew together in a frown, but before the shadow of it touched her eyes she remembered where she was and jerked up into a sitting position. The movement made her head throb and she groaned and put her hand to her temples.

"You're lucky you haven't got more than a headache," a male voice said. "As it is, your leg's going to be a beautiful shade of blue."

Gingerly straightening again, Nicola looked to see who had spoken, and found herself staring into quizzical, light grey eyes.

"Who are *you*?" she asked.

"Barnaby Grayson. I run this place."

She looked around her, noticing the hard settee on which she was lying, the red Turkey carpet on the floor scuffed by age to show bare patches, and the large desk – piled high with papers – that stood in front of a green-curtained window. Despite its shabbiness the room had a welcoming air, due she surmised both to the bright coal fire burning in an old-fashioned grate and to the equally warming presence of the tall, loose-limbed man standing opposite her, a foot on the fender, an arm propped on the mantelpiece.

Though not quite as shabby as his surroundings, he fitted in with them very well, his grey slacks – though clean and well pressed – shining with age, and his cashmere sweater as thin around the elbows as the carpet on which he was standing. The glow of the firelight lent colour to his face, though as he half-turned from it to look at her she saw that his skin was tanned, with a faint stubble on his square chin, as though he had not shaved with much care. Dark eyebrows, unusually well-shaped for a man, marked his eyes, but his brown hair was soft and unruly and glinted with an unmistakable red as it caught the glare of the bulb above his head.

"What sort of centre *is* this?" she asked.

"A place where people like you can come for help."

"Like me?" she said in surprise.

"Yes." He seemed amused by her tone. "You can't deny you look as if you need some!"

His eyes moved over her and only then did she become aware of the tattered wisps of material that clung to her body.

"My — my dress, you mean," she stammered. "What's wrong with it?"

"It's hardly what the well-dressed girl is wearing this season!" he chided. "You needn't be ashamed of being poor. It happens to the best of us."

Nicola lowered her eyes hastily, suddenly understanding him. He believed her costume was for real! A vague memory of his voice before she had fainted returned to her. Hadn't he said something about her being a Cinderella?

"I've been to a party," she explained.

"For hoboes, no doubt!"

Angry that he did not believe her, she swung her feet to the ground. The room turned gently on its axis and she bit tightly on to her lower lip until the walls steadied.

"Drink this," he ordered, and came towards her with a glass.

She smelt brandy and shook her head, but ignoring the ges-

13

ture he put the tumbler against her teeth. "It'll make you feel better. Drink it."

The liquid burned her throat and she coughed and pushed the glass away. "I hate brandy! Don't you have any champagne?" she said without thinking.

"Only on Leap Year!" He squatted down so that his eyes were level with hers. "Why all the pretence? Everyone in this house is in the same boat as you; that's why they came here in the first place."

"You too?"

He straightened. "I'm in a slightly different position. I told you — I run the Centre."

Steadied by the brandy, she stood up, realising crossly that she was barefoot. "What's happened to my shoes?"

He moved back to the hearth and lifted up a pair of shabby pumps. They had been loaned to her by her maid, in place of the satin ones she had intended to wear.

Snatching them from him, she put them on. They made little difference to her height, and even standing as straight as she could the top of her head barely reached his chin, so that she was forced to tilt her head back to look at him. "What time is it?" she asked.

"After midnight."

"I must go."

"I'm not letting you wander off into the night."

"You can't stop me. I'm going home."

"You told Miss Thomas you couldn't go home." He caught her shoulder. "Be a good girl and sit down again. Joanna's rustling up something to eat. It won't be much at this time of night, I'm afraid, but it should stop the pangs of hunger." One eyebrow lifted. "I take it you *are* hungry. You look as if you hadn't had a square meal in months."

"I'm naturally small," she replied, and felt herself colouring

14

at the intensity of his gaze. This ridiculous man really believed she was a down-and-out! It would be laughable if it weren't rather touching. That anyone should believe – even for a single moment – that Nicola Rosten was a homeless waif! Yet if a home meant a family and love, then she was indeed homeless. Tears stung her eyes and angrily she brushed them away. Why on earth was she so jumpy?

"Being knocked down by a car is no joke," the man said, as though sensing her emotional turmoil. "It really would be advisable for you to stay here tonight. You won't be under any obligation to stay longer. You'll be free to leave in the morning."

She hesitated, then in her usual impulsive way made a decision. "All right, I'll stay." She sat down on the settee, jumping sharply as a spring dug into her. "Is everything old and broken here?" she demanded.

"Most of it's old, but it's not all broken! I've been meaning to get that settee repaired."

"You're too busy, I suppose?"

He nodded equably, and she felt her quick surge of temper ebb.

"How many –" she paused, searching for the right word. "How many residents do you have here?"

"We try not to have any permanents," he replied. "We like to get people settled in jobs and digs as quickly as we can. But thirty-five is our capacity. We're almost full at the moment."

Before she could ask any more questions a young woman – a few years older than herself – came in with a tray. She was tall and slim, and her tweed skirt and a matching wool blouse gave authority to her appearance.

"Joanna, this is –" the man looked at Nicola. "I don't know your name."

15

"Nic –" She thought fast. "Nicky Rose."

"Welcome to the Centre, Nicky," Joanna said, putting the tray on the desk. Her voice was as cool as the look in her hard brown eyes, though they grew warmer as they rested on the man. "I've brought you some supper too, Barnaby. You ate nothing tonight."

"I was busy talking."

"You should relax at meal times."

"I can't. It's the only chance I get to see everybody here."

The girl gave an angry sniff and walked out, and the man moved to the desk. "Will you eat over here, Nicky, or have it on your lap?"

"I'll come over," she said, and doing so, stared in dismay at two mugs of cocoa and several thick slices of bread and butter and jam. "Is this what *you're* eating too?"

"Of course. Why not?"

"I thought you'd have something special – after all, you do run this place."

"I don't think that would be fair," he smiled. "If I didn't have the same food I'd have to eat on my own."

"Would that be so awful?"

"I prefer to eat with everyone else. Then people can see me and talk to me any time they like."

"It doesn't sound much of a life."

"It's the one I chose."

"Do you wear a hair shirt too?"

He chuckled and held out the plate of bread.

Masking her distaste, she took a slice and forced herself to bite into it. She was unexpectedly hungry and remembered that her discovery of Jeffrey and Deborah had made her miss the buffet. It was hours since she had last eaten.

"I'd give anything for a steak," she murmured, and bit back the rest of her words as she saw his expression.

16

"I'm afraid we don't run to steak here," he said gently. "But I can promise you won't go hungry."

Annoyed at her runaway tongue, she picked up the mug of cocoa. It was too strong and too sweet and after a couple of sips she set it back on the tray.

The man did not seem to find his unpalatable and drained the cup to the last drop, looking at her half-full one admonishingly. "Drink it up, it's made with milk."

"I hate milk."

"It'll do you good."

"I hate eating things because they'll do me good – and I hate people who want to *do* good!"

"You must lead a pretty hateful life!"

"On the contrary. There aren't that many do-gooders in the world! Most people only care about themselves."

He moved back to stand in front of the fireplace, hands in the pockets of his trousers. "You're very cynical for a kid."

"I'm twenty-one."

"You look younger."

"How old are *you*?" she demanded.

He was surprised by her question, and she realised it must be unusual for a recipient of generosity to question the giver of it. But after a slight pause he answered her. "I'm thirty-three. Old and ancient to the likes of you."

"I like older men," she said. "Marty's sixty and –"

"Marty?" The sharp question made her realise that once again her tongue had run away with her.

"A friend of mine," she said hastily. "I met him when I – at the last place I worked."

"What did you do?"

"I was a ladies' maid." She said the first thing that came into her mind, and was unprepared for his sudden shout of laughter.

17

"You don't expect me to believe *that*!"

"I don't see why not!" She tossed her head. "You need to be very skilful, you know. You have to sew clothes and do hair and make-up. I'm interested in things like that."

"Why did you lose your job?"

"What makes you think I lost it?"

He caught his breath and began again. "Why did you leave your job, then?"

Crossing her fingers, she said: "The girl I worked for was too – too bossy. She went to parties nearly every night and expected me to wait up for her. I rarely got to bed before three. I wouldn't have minded if she'd appreciated it, but she was spoiled and took everything for granted."

"Most rich girls do!"

"Do you know many?"

"None."

"I'm sure that's helped you to form an opinion."

He glanced at her sharply, but she kept her expression artless and he relaxed. "What did you do after you left your job?" he asked.

She paused, wondering what her own maid Maria would do in similar circumstances. Probably take the appreciable amount of money she had saved and return to find a young man in Italy! But this was not the answer to give the man in front of her. Her eyes roamed the room and came to rest on the tray. "I was a waitress," she said brightly, "but it was terribly hard work."

"You've been out of a job a long while, haven't you?"

"Why do you say that?"

"From the way you're dressed. No one would go around like that if they could afford better."

Her mouth twitched and she lowered her eyes quickly.

"Don't cry," he said unexpectedly, and for the second time

18

that evening put his hand on her shoulder. "I suggest you go to bed and get a good night's sleep. We can talk again in the morning and you can let me know if you'd like to stay on."

"I *am* rather tired," she admitted, glad to end the catechism, and followed him out of the room to the hall.

Looking at it with clearer eyes she saw that several rooms led off from each side, as well as a staircase going down to what was obviously a basement, and another leading up several floors to the bedrooms.

Beckoning her forward, Barnaby Grayson went up to the first floor and along a linoleum-covered corridor to a room at the end. He knocked on the door and opened it, then stood aside for her to enter.

Nicola did so and saw four beds, three of them occupied. A girl in one of them lifted her head and then with a grunt fell back against the pillow.

Nicola stepped back into the corridor so hurriedly that she bumped against the man. "I'm not going to sleep in there!" she said vehemently.

"Why not?"

"*Why not?*" Words failed her. "Because I'm not used to sharing a room with anyone," she said at last. "That's why not!"

"I'm afraid all the suites are occupied," came the sardonic answer.

"Then I'll go." She marched down the stairs to the hall and stood there shivering until he came abreast of her. "What have you done with my fur?"

Without a word he went into the sitting-room and returned with a limp, mud-stained stole that bore no relation to the glossy mink it had been earlier that evening.

Without comment she took it from him and wrapped it round her, unaware of the pathetic picture she made in her tattered dress, with her large eyes glittering like jewels in her pale face.

"You just need a tray and you'd be the original match-girl!" he grinned involuntarily.

"Are you always so rude to the people you're supposed to help?" she snapped.

"Only when they throw my help back in my face!"

His remark caught her by surprise, and she hesitated. "I'm sorry, I didn't mean to be rude. But I can't share a room with so many strangers. It makes me — makes me nervous."

"Where will you go?"

On the point of saying "Home", she stopped, and instead opened the front door. Fog billowed like smoke and the man behind her reached out and banged it shut again.

"It's impossible for you to leave," he said flatly. "You can't see a hand in front of you."

"I'm not your responsibility."

"You are while you're here."

"Then let me go!"

He frowned, looking down at her from what seemed a great height. "You'd better sleep with me."

"How dare you!"

For an instant he looked taken aback, then his firm but well-cut mouth creased into a smile. "You *have* got a nasty mind! But I meant the offer literally. Sleep — not sex!"

Unused to such blunt speaking — the young men in her circle were frequently flirtatious, occasionally passionate, but rarely so bluntly matter-of-fact — she felt her cheeks flame. "Thanks for the distinction, Mr. Grayson, but I don't want to *sleep* with you either."

"Well, I've no intention of letting you leave." He took a deep breath. "For heaven's sake, be sensible. It's already past one o'clock and I've an early call in the morning."

Catching her arm, he propelled her purposefully behind the stair well and through an alcove into what appeared to be an annexe. Here several more rooms led off a white-painted corridor, and he pushed her into the one at the end.

Austerely furnished – he seemed determined to make no concession to himself merely because he ran the place, Nicola decided – this room was nonetheless more pleasant than the others she had seen. White walls were given colour by large, unframed oil-paintings, one of which acted as headboard for a narrow bed, its navy blue counterpane contrasting with the dark red curtains and large square rug that covered the floor.

"You're fond of red carpets," she remarked, keeping her eyes away from the bed.

"Beggars can't be choosers," he said cheerfully. "All the rugs in the house come from one of our benefactors, and she had a penchant for red!"

"Or a hatred – maybe that's why she gave them to you!" Nicola pointed to the walls. "Are the paintings yours?"

"A gift from someone we helped," he said vaguely, and advanced towards her. "You'd better get undressed."

"No, thank you."

"You can't sleep in your dress, it's soaking. Take it off."

She shook her head, and his expression became so angry that she backed away. The hard edge of a narrow settee dug into her calves, and she sat abruptly down on it before her shaking limbs made it obvious that she had to do so.

"You may have been able to prevent me leaving here, Mr. Grayson, but you can't force me to undress – not if I have to share your bedroom!"

"I'd have suggested you slept in the sitting-room, except that we like to keep it free in case anyone comes into the house during the night. That way there's always somewhere for them to doss down. It's the only reason I offered to share my room with you. I also like to sleep alone, Miss Rose, and I assure you I've no designs on your virtue!" He crossed to a chest of drawers, took out a pair of pale blue pyjamas and draped them on her lap. "Get into these."

"You're very kind," she murmured, touching the jacket. "I thought you meant me to – to –"

"Sleep in the nude?" His laugh was dry. "It wouldn't matter to me if you did. I'm used to women's bodies."

"You talk as if you've seen a lot."

"I have," he confessed. "Hundreds."

Disbelieving, she stared at him. "Aren't you ashamed of making a remark like that?"

"Why should I be? I'll probably see hundreds more."

"And loving them all, no doubt," she said scornfully.

"Love's too strong an emotion. Interest is more like it."

With an angry exclamation she stood up, clutching the pyjamas in her arms. The joke she had begun so lightheartedly was wearing thin, and the thought of her house in Belgravia and her own bedroom was infinitely inviting.

"Please let me go," she pleaded.

"In the morning. For tonight you're staying here."

"I've no intention of sharing your bed."

"I'm glad to hear it. That will save me from declining your offer!" He bent to the settee and tugged at its back. It glided down to form a narrow but adequate divan. Still without a word he went over to an old-fashioned wardrobe and from its base took out a pillow and some blankets. "I'm sure you can make this up for yourself," he said, dumping them down and going to the door. "I'll be back in five minutes. You'd better be in bed by then."

"The b-bathroom," she stammered. "Where is it?"

"The door next to the wardrobe."

"So you do treat yourself differently, after all," she could not help retorting.

He walked out, a slight smile his only acknowledgement of her sarcasm. For a moment she stood in the centre of the room considering his behaviour. She had never met a man like him before; he must be a social worker of some sort. She pulled a face. She had always run a mile from those sort of people. They usually did that kind of work to compensate for their own inadequacies or guilt complex. Not that Barnaby Grayson seemed either inadequate or guilty! Barnaby. What an old-fashioned name it was. A bit like the man himself, in his time-less sweater and baggy slacks.

A sound outside the door made her realise that a couple of minutes from the five he had allotted her had already gone, and knowing he would come into the room at the end of that time whether she had undressed or not, she ran into the bath-room.

And she had accused him of giving himself an additional luxury, she thought, looking at the utilitarian shower – a tap in the ceiling – and a large mottled sink below an equally mottled mirror. His own bathroom. Her maid would not even have deigned to use such a place!

Hurriedly she washed, slipped out of her rags – custom-made by the Queen's own dressmaker – and into the pyjamas. They fell around her like swaddling clothes, the jacket being long enough to serve as a nightshirt. Looping the trouser belt twice around her waist and rolling up the legs, she padded back into the room and hurriedly made up the bed. She was just folding the blankets when he came in.

"That's better," he said jovially. "Now hop in. I shan't be a minute before I turn out the light." He disappeared into the bathroom, looking strangely different as he returned in dark gold pyjamas. They were unexpectedly resplendent, piped

23

with white and with a monogram on the breast pocket. "They're not really me," he said with a slight smile, showing his awareness of her thoughts. "They were somebody's way of saying a special thank-you."

"From one of the hundreds of bodies you've seen?"

"Actually, it's one body I haven't seen." He climbed into bed and switched off the bedside lamp.

In the darkness the room took on a new shape. The edge of the wardrobe loomed large, the glimmer of its mirrored centre-panel reflecting the moonlight that seeped through the closed curtains; the bulky shape of the desk seemed a long way away, while the end of Barnaby Grayson's bed appeared to be much closer.

A spring creaked and her heart pounded, her body gripped by fear.

"Relax, Nicky," Barnaby's voice, disembodied, was deep and whimsical. "I've never gone in for rape!"

Furious that he had guessed her fright, she lost her fear. "I'm glad," she said icily. "I'd hate to join the legion!"

A chuckle was her only answer, and she turned on her side and pulled the rough blanket around her. Hundreds of bodies! What a thing to admit. What a story this would make to tell everyone tomorrow. Suddenly she remembered Jeffrey, amazed that she hadn't thought of him for the last hour. Jeffrey, whom she had been going to marry until he had shown himself to be of the same calibre as the other young men she had known. Marty was right; she was an awful judge of men. But perhaps there weren't many nice ones around. Hundreds of women, indeed, she thought again, and then abruptly fell asleep.

CHAPTER THREE

Where on earth was Maria with her hot lemon juice? Nicola thought tiredly, and stretching herself in bed found one of her feet dangling over the edge. Startled, for her bed was six feet wide, she sat up. Only then did she remember she was in a hostel near the Embankment. She stared across at the other bed in the corner. It had been smoothly made and gave no indication of having been occupied. She looked for her watch and realised she didn't have one. As Cinderella she had worn no jewellery, not even her engagement ring, lest it spoil the charade.

Not that Jeffrey had worried about spoiling *his* act. Her blond Prince Charming had decided to *play* the part of Casanova as well as to dress like one. And it was a good thing he had. At last he had shown her what he was before it was too late. Sighing heavily, she got out of bed.

In the daylight the bathroom was even more dilapidated than it had been at first sight, and with some trepidation she stood under the shower and switched on the taps. Tepid water trickled over her and she hurriedly washed, wrapped herself in a skimpy bath towel – how unlike her own thick fleecy ones at home – and returned to the bedroom to look for her dress.

All her clothes had vanished, and she was peering half-heartedly around the room when Barnaby Grayson came in. In yellow sweater and brown slacks he looked younger than last night, his skin glowing pink, his hair thick and unruly.

"So you're up," he said by way of greeting. "How do you feel?"

"Naked without my clothes. Where are they?"

"I gave them to Joanna. One of the girls will take them to the cleaners with the rest of our things. We send a sackful down each week."

"You had no right to take them. I've nothing else to wear!"

"You couldn't put that dress on again," he said gently. "It's in rags."

"It's meant to be in rags!"

He grinned, and she realised how silly her remark must sound to someone who did not know it was a fancy dress costume.

"There's something I'd like to tell you," she began, and stopped as a sharp knock at the door heralded the entry of Joanna Morgan. She looked as practical in the daylight as she had done the evening before, though her tweed skirt had been replaced by a navy dress with white collar and cuffs. An attractive girl, Nicola decided, if you like your women serious. And the man beside her obviously liked them no matter *what* they wore. It would be difficult to keep up one's standards in the face of so many conquests.

"I hope these will fit you," Joanna said, and put a bundle of clothes into Nicola's unresisting arms. "They may be a bit on the big side, but they were the smallest we could find." She looked at Barnaby. "Coming down for breakfast?"

He smiled and joined her, glancing over his shoulder at Nicola. "Get dressed and come down to the kitchen."

Nicola nodded and, as soon as she was alone, slipped into the clothes she had been given. They were clean, which was the only thing to be said in their favour. For the rest, they were too dark, too bulky and several sizes too big: the skirt shapeless and reaching halfway down her calves, the sweater an unbecoming shade of grey. If Barnaby Grayson's assistant had wanted to find the most unflattering clothes, she couldn't have chosen better, for that they *had* been chosen deliberately Nicola was convinced.

Leaving the bedroom, she headed for the front door. But halfway towards it she stopped. It was silly to leave without having a cup of coffee, and she must also thank the people here for their hospitality. Believing her to be destitute, they had shown kindness and compassion; the least she could do was to thank them.

Following a tantalising smell of bacon, she went down a flight of steps to the basement, and the large old-fashioned kitchen where several people were eating around a well-scrubbed wooden table.

Barnaby Grayson was seated between two young girls; though dissimilar in colour and features they had the same stamp of poverty, with lank hair and greyish skins; but they appeared high-spirited and were chatting to him with uninhibited friendliness.

At Nicola's entry he waved an arm and motioned her to find herself a seat. Almost at once someone set a place of bacon and egg in front of her. Used to thin, curling strips of bacon served hot and crisp on fine-boned china, she stared distastefully at the dried-up edges of the bacon set before her, and even more distastefully at the overcooked eggs. Picking up a steel fork, she made a pretence of eating. Surprisingly it was tasty, or perhaps she was too hungry to mind that it wasn't, and she quickly cleared her plate. Opposite her Barnaby Grayson was being commandeered by the girl on his right-hand side, whose dingy yellow hair was an almost perfect match for her skin.

"Even if I do take the job," she was saying, "I don't know if I'll stick it for long."

"You stuck your last one for two months," he reminded her. "And that was one month longer than the job before!"

The girl laughed, the sound turning into a cough that made

27

her shoulders heave, but brought a becoming flush to her cheeks. "Go on," she said defiantly to the man beside her when she could catch her breath. "Why don't you tell me to stop smoking?"

"I try not to be obvious!" He pushed back his chair. "Come to my room and let me have a look at you."

He walked out and the girl followed. Nicola set down her tea and watched them bleakly. How could he be so obvious? And so early in the morning too!

There was a movement close by and she saw that Joanna had taken the vacant chair beside her. "The clothes look nice on you," she smiled.

"You must be joking. I feel like the Wreck of the Heperus."

"They're better than the one you wore when you arrived," came the quiet reprimand. "You should be grateful."

"Is that why you work here?" Nicola asked. "Because you want gratitude?"

"Certainly not!" Colour rose in the smooth cheeks. "I'm sorry if I've annoyed you. I didn't mean to."

Yes, you did, Nicola thought to herself, and wondered why this confident-looking girl should be antagonistic towards her.

Joanna's next words gave her the reason. "Barnaby told me you wouldn't share a room with any of the other girls. He should have woken me up. You could easily have used the divan in my room."

"I didn't want to share *anybody's* room," Nicola retorted. "I wanted to leave, but he wouldn't let me."

"Naturally he wouldn't. You'd been knocked down and were suffering from shock." The hard brown eyes looked into hers. "I hope you're feeling better."

"I'm fine. I had a perfect night – even though I swam

28

around in Barnaby's pyjamas."

Joanna gave an exclamation. "He *knows* we always keep extra pyjamas in the linen room. It wasn't at all necessary for him to give you *his*."

"Perhaps he wanted me to have them," Nicola joked, and was surprised by the fury her remark aroused.

"He's too generous," the girl snapped. "He always lets women take advantage of him."

"I'd have thought it was the other way around."

"What's that supposed to mean?"

"I know your Mr. Do-Gooder's reputation. He told me about it himself."

"What on earth are you talking about?"

Wishing she had not started the conversation, Nicola decided to end it quickly. "He's a self-confessed Lothario. Hundreds of women's bodies, was the way he put it." She stood up. "I won't wait for my dress to come back. If I could borrow the clothes I'm wearing, I'll see they're returned to you later today."

She was at the front door when Joanna caught up with her.

"You seem to be under a misapprehension about Barnaby," the girl said. "Either he doesn't make himself clear or you misunderstood him."

"I know what he said."

"But not what he meant. Of course he's seen hundreds of women's bodies. He did gynaecology before he became a psychiatrist."

It seemed an endless span of time before the words held any meaning for Nicola, then as they did, she went scarlet. "You mean he's a *doctor*?"

"I thought you knew."

Nicola shook her head and plunged headlong towards the

room where she had been taken on her arrival. Luckily it was empty, and she closed the door and leaned on it, waiting for her heart to stop pounding. No wonder she had had the feeling that Barnaby Grayson had been laughing at her! He *had* been laughing; deliberately, teasingly, he had led her to believe he was little better than a Bluebeard. How dared he hide the fact that he was a doctor? Barnaby Grayson, he had said when she had asked his name, carefully omitting to add the all-important prefix. What a beast he was!

Remembering the amused glance he had flung her this morning when he had left the room with the long-haired blonde, Nicola grew hot with indignation. He must have known what her thoughts had been – and why shouldn't he when he had encouraged her to think them?

The door moved and she stepped back as it opened to disclose the man himself. Looking at him with seeing eyes she admitted that only the shock of Jeffrey's infidelity, coupled with being knocked down by a car, could have robbed her of the ability to recognise Barnaby Grayson's command and the authority which sat so easily on his shoulders.

"Why didn't you tell me you were a doctor?" she demanded.

He smiled slightly. "I hadn't realised you didn't know until you jumped on me last night when I said I'd –"

"Why didn't you tell me then?" she interrupted, face flaming.

"It seemed a joke."

"At my expense!"

"Surely it wasn't all that important?"

"It was to me. I had to share a room with you."

"You weren't really frightened, were you? You must have dossed down in some pretty odd places in your time."

She positively shook with anger. "How dare you say a thing

like that? Don't you have any respect for my feelings?"

"I only respect the truth," he said quietly, "and that's something you're running away from. Ever since you met me you've been pretending – putting on an act that's stupid and unnecessary."

She fell back a step. "You mean you – you *know* who I am?"

"Of course." He led her, unresisting, to the lumpy settee. "You're down on your luck and trying to pretend you're not. You obviously haven't had a job for months and you must have pawned most of your clothes. You wouldn't have worn that flimsy dress last night if you'd had anything warmer. It's foolish to put on an act, Nicky. I can't begin to help you until you start being honest with yourself."

Her thoughts were too chaotic to make verbal sense and she was still wondering how to answer him when he continued. "If I had told you last night that I was a doctor, you'd have run away like a startled rabbit. Anyway, *you* were so busy lying to *me*, I felt you deserved a few back in return!"

"I still think it was despicable of you." Once again she was the imperious Nicola Rosten.

"My, my," he drawled, "we *are* Miss High Society this morning!"

"I am," she flared.

"And I'm the King of Siam!" He shook her none too gently. "Grow up, Nicky; daydreams are fine when you're a child, but they can be dangerous when you grow up."

"I know the difference between fantasy and reality," she retorted.

"I'm sure you do. But you obviously find fantasy more satisfying. Not that I blame you." His face was unexpectedly gentle. "You don't look as if you've had an easy time. You're as thin as a rake."

Nicola lowered her eyes to hide their amusement. Anyone

31

would look thin in a sweater three sizes too large. Not even the curves of Mae West would be visible through the bulk of this triple-knit. So she was running away from reality, was she? So she looked as though life had treated her badly, did she? How sure he was that he was right – and what pleasure it would give her to throw all his words back into his insufferable face!

"Why not stay here for a few days and see how things go?" he broke into her thoughts. "I'm here every evening for you to talk to if you wish, and during the day there's always Joanna and Mrs. Thomas."

"What do *you* do during the day?" she hedged.

"I work at the hospital. I started this hostel in my spare time."

"It belongs to everyone who comes here," he said quietly.

"You mean its *yours*?"

"It can belong to you too, if you want to take advantage of it."

She thought of Jeffrey and the other young men she had unwisely loved. "I'm more used to people taking advantage of *me*."

"That won't happen here. Make a fresh start, Nicky. You've nothing to lose."

"Will *you* help me?" she asked softly.

"That's what I'm here for."

Again she lowered her eyes, fighting the temptation to have her moment of triumph now. Yet how much sweeter it would be if she could wait and give him more words to eat than those already in store for him."

"Well?" he asked. "Will you stay?"

"Yes, Dr. Grayson." She raised limpid hazel eyes to his. "I'll put myself entirely in your hands."

His grey eyes looked back at her with such intensity that for a brief instant she had the feeling he could read her thoughts.

But when he spoke it was only to say he was sure she was doing the wisest thing, and that he would see her later, when he returned from the hospital.

Only when he had left the room did she do a little dance around it, giggling to herself as she looked ahead to the next week; seven days should give her enough time to run a ring around Doctor Do-Good Grayson! Breathless from her exertions, she fell back on to the settee, uncaring of the lumpy springs, her mind still savouring the pleasure ahead.

After a few minutes she stood up and wandered round the room. A large table near the window was stacked with old magazines and dog-eared books, none of which she found appealing, and apart from yesterday's newspaper there was nothing for her to read. Nothing, indeed, for her to do.

She yawned and stretched her arms. She felt she had been up for hours, yet an old clock on the mantelpiece only showed half-past nine. Normally at this time she would be sitting up in bed sipping her orange juice, while Maria ran her bath and set out fresh, pure silk lingerie. A far cry from the tepid shower and cotton underclothes that *this* new day had brought her! But it would all be worth it in the end: Barnaby Grayson's face would see to that!

Wandering over to an old-fashioned-looking wireless that stood on another table, she switched it on. An ominous crackle filled the air, but a twist of the knob brought forth a programme for schools and some church music, neither of which was appropriate to her mood. Used to a wireless which at the flick of a button brought in America as clearly as London, she turned the switch off irritably. There was a snap and, dismayed, she saw it had come away in her hand.

"Drat it!" she exclaimed.

"Is anything wrong?" It was Joanna Morgan, her look of enquiry changing to crossness as she saw what had happened.

33

"Couldn't you be more careful? Now you've broken it."

"It was an accident."

"You seem prone to accidents," commented Joanna dryly.

"What does that mean?"

"It was an accident that brought you here."

"I didn't arrange it," Nicola replied, "though it turned out to be a lucky one for me." Aware of the unresponsive look on Joanna Morgan's face, she said sweetly: "Are *you* here to help too – like Barnaby?"

"We're all here to help." The reply was stiff and unfriendly. "I'm a psychologist."

"Have you always done this sort of work?"

"I was in industry until a year ago. Then I met Barnaby – Dr. Grayson – and he persuaded me to come here."

"I should have thought you'd prefer industrial work. You don't look the type to enjoy helping down-and-outs."

"It can be frustrating," Joanna Morgan said coolly. "But it's extremely rewarding when one achieves results."

"Is Barnaby successful?" Nicola asked, more for want of something to say than because she cared.

"*Dr.* Grayson," there was notable emphasis on the prefix, "has achieved remarkable success in his particular field."

"You make him sound like a farmer!"

"An apt remark when you consider that he encourages people to grow and develop."

Feeling she had been successfully put in her place, Nicola retired into herself, a habit she had developed when – as a child – her eager curiosity about the world around her had elicited a dampening response from her current nurse or governess. I had all the money in the world, she thought suddenly, but no one to talk with.

"As you'll be staying here a little while," the psychologist was foremost in Joanna Morgan now, "there are a few things I'd like to know for the record."

"I haven't got a record," Nicola retorted. "I'm not a criminal."

"Please don't misunderstand me," Joanna flushed and looked – to Nicola's eye – irritatingly pretty. "All I meant was that Dr. Grayson likes to know the reason why a person comes here, and how each one progresses."

"Is he planning to write a book on it? It's bound to be a success – those sort of books usually are." Nicola warmed to the subject. "I can just see it on the best-seller list. *How I Helped The Drop-outs Get Back Their Self-respect.* It's amazing the pleasure that well-fed liberals get from reading about people like me!"

"I can understand you feeling bitter towards society. But you shouldn't be suspicious of everyone." Joanna's words were sympathetic, but her face was not, and Nicola wondered if she was unduly sensitive to the girl. If not, then she couldn't see Joanna having much success with this work. After only a few hours she was beginning to know the person it required: someone who could be authoritative without being bossy; who could display intelligence without arrogance.

"If you'll come into the office," Joanna interrupted Nicola's thoughts, "I'll give you your list of jobs. Dr. Grayson doesn't like people being idle here unless there's a good reason for it."

"Like death, I suppose? I should think that's the *only* reason that would qualify in *his* mind!"

With a sniff of disapprobation the older girl led the way into a small office directly opposite Barnaby Grayson's bedroom. It was filled with filing cabinets, a battered desk and an equally battered typewriter. Joanna Morgan began to search through some papers and Nicola watched. In the daylight she looked younger than she had done the night before; not more than twenty-five, though with a serious manner that made her appear older. Her clothes, though formal, did not hide a very good figure that was in no way depreciated by a classically oval face with pale but clear skin and well-shaped features. It was difficult to define in what way she just missed being beautiful. Perhaps it was the stiff control with which she did everything or the hardness that not even a smile could totally remove from her face. It's the eyes, Nicola finally decided, they're like brown pebbles.

"Here we are," Joanna held out a typewritten sheet of paper. "Several of the girls are having to double-up on some of the work, so if you could take over one of the jobs . . ."

Nicola leaned forward to look at the list and felt Joanna stiffen, as if she had to restrain herself from moving away. Perhaps she thinks I might smell, Nicola thought, and could not resist saying: "My clothes are perfectly clean, Miss Morgan. You gave them to me yourself."

The girl reddened, but training came to her rescue and silently she put the list on the desk.

Looking at it, Nicola nearly changed her mind about staying here, but sensing that this was exactly what Joanna wanted, she pushed the idea out of her mind.

"I'm very good at sewing," she said. "That's down here as a job."

Joanna glanced at the list. "It's being done by Elaine Evans and it's her only job. Look at the girls who are doing two, and take one of those."

Nicola studied the list again. It was less than inspiring, with cooking, dishwashing, shopping and ironing noticeably understaffed. "I'll have a go at the shopping," she said, thinking it would at least get her out of the hostel for a few hours at a time.

"I'm afraid you can't do that. Shopping requires money and we don't give our new residents any cash until Dr. Grayson says so."

Nicola stiffened with shock. "I'm not a thief!"

"No one's suggesting you are. It's just one of the rules."

"It's crazy! If I came here with the intention of stealing money I wouldn't be so obvious about it."

"If you have any comment to make on the subject, I suggest you take it up with Dr. Grayson." Joanna looked at the list again. "I believe you've been a ladies' maid and also a waitress. Surely you could help with the dishwashing and ironing?"

Instinctively Nicola knew she was expected to refuse. "Suits me," she said laconically. "It'll really be home from home then!"

"You might as well start now." Joanna held the door open and Nicola preceded her back into the corridor and down to the basement.

The kitchen had been cleared of breakfast and three girls were busy preparing meat and a huge amount of cabbage and potatoes.

"You'll find the ironing board and the washing in the cupboard," Joanna said, and waited while Nicola took out a heavy board behind which was stacked a mountain of sheets and pillowcases.

"I'm not expected to iron all this?"

"We don't run to an electric ironer," came the cool reply.

"What's wrong with the laundry?"

"Price if you're complaining about what you have to do . . ."

"I'm only commenting," Nicola said quickly, and reached into the cupboard for the iron. This, at least, seemed new and manageable, and she plugged it into a socket in the wall beside her and then carefully hoisted a sheet on to the ironing board. Three-quarters of it dragged on the floor, and Joanna clicked her lips disapprovingly.

"Fold the sheet, Nicky. There's no point ironing it and then having to re-wash it."

One of the other girls giggled, and feeling inept, Nicola manfully struggled with the folds. It was impossible to keep the sheet off the ground, and her movements were made more clumsy by knowing she was being watched.

"I can manage on my own, Miss Morgan," she said in dulcet tones. "There's at least two days' work for me here."

"You won't be able to do it the whole day. You'll have to give a hand with the washing up."

"That'll be a welcome diversion from ironing."

Joanna's eyes flickered, but without any answering humour, she turned and walked out.

Immediately the three girls grinned at Nicola and introduced themselves. "Don't let Joanna worry you," the eldest of the trio – Carole Stritch – said. "She's nice when you get to know her."

"She takes things too seriously," the youngest of the three said in a pronounced Midland accent.

"You're not forced to work set hours either," added the third girl, the lank-haired blonde who had commandeered Barnaby Grayson's attention after breakfast that morning. "Joanna makes out we can only stay here as long as we pull out our fingers, but Barnaby says we needn't work if we don't want to."

"Fat chance you'd have of staying here if you didn't," Carole said. "The trouble with you is you believe everything Barnaby says."

"I don't."

"You do," said Carole, and added a profane word more by

38

way of endearment than anger.

"Don't you call him Doctor?" Nicola said hastily.

Carole laughed. "You must be kidding! He couldn't care less what we call him, so long as he thinks he's getting through to us."

"Is he?"

"Not as far as I'm concerned. I stay here because the grub's good, the bed's clean, and the place is warm. Come summer and I'll be off again."

"Is it as simple as that?" Nicola was unable to hide her surprise. "I thought this was a sort of clinic."

"So it is, but there are no rules here. You can leave when you like and you can come back too — providing they've got room."

"You'd better make your reservation for next winter, then," said the lank-haired blonde.

"I might not be in England," Carole shrugged. "I fancy hitching to India." She resumed her pounding of the mince-meat, arms flailing as though she were enjoying the expenditure of energy.

Nicole began to iron, laboriously ensuring that the sheet remained on the ironing board, a feat which soon became an impossibility. She had never ironed anything in her life before, though she had occasionally gone into Maria's sewing room and watched her at work. It was a pity she had not taken more notice of how it was done. At least she might have learned how to control a cotton sheet.

She was glad when a break was caused by lunch — ham and mashed potatoes with the inevitable bread and butter and mugs of tea. Twenty people crowded into the kitchen for it, squeezing round the table and helping themselves liberally. Their departure left a mound of dishes to be washed and dried, and though the lank-haired blonde helped her, it was well into the afternoon before Nicola was finished.

"I'm off to my session," the girl said.

"What session?"

"Barnaby's." The tone expressed surprise at Nicola's ignorance, and reluctant to compound it further by questioning, she watched in silence as the girl dropped her apron on the table and raced out of the room.

Heaving a sigh of relief at being alone, Nicola dried her hands on a damp tea towel and dropped exhaustedly on to a chair. Three hours' ironing and an hour at the sink had left her more enervated than a whole night spent dancing at a discothèque. She stared at her hands – red and wrinkled from the soapy water. The masquerade was fast losing its amusement. One more dirty dish and she'd walk out right now. She re-activated her flagging spirits by rehearsing what she would say to Barnaby Grayson when the time came, and then gave herself an additional fillip by envisaging Joanna Morgan's reaction too.

There was a clatter of steps down the stairs, and anticipating one of the people she had met at lunch, she did not move. But it was Barnaby Grayson who came into the kitchen, looking unexpectedly austere in a navy suit.

"I know," he said with a slight smile before she could speak. "I'm too late for lunch and too early for tea."

"You mean you haven't eaten?"

"Too busy." As he spoke he filled the kettle and set it to boil, then disappeared into the larder, coming back with the remnants of the ham, some slices of bread and butter liberally covered with jam, and a lump of pickle.

"For a doctor you're not very protein-conscious," she commented, as he started to eat.

"I had egg and bacon for breakfast," he replied, "and I'll be eating dinner."

The kettle began to sing and she moved over to make the tea. Water splattered on the stove as she filled the teapot. She dropped the teaspoon to the floor and splashed milk in the saucer.

"Not very domesticated, are you?" he said pleasantly, looking at the leaves swimming gaily on the surface of the tea she set before him.

"I've got other qualifications," she snapped, and seeing the way he raised his eyebrows, she went scarlet. "I don't mean those sort."

At once the humour left his face. "Why do you always think I'm standing in judgment? I told you, Nicky, once you're accepted here, your past is forgotten."

"Can people forget their past so easily?"

"Some can."

"And those that can't?"

"They need different help."

"What sort of help do *I* need?" she asked lightly.

"I'm not sure. I don't like making off-the-cuff judgments. It might help if you came along to our sessions though. I think you'd enjoy them."

"What do you do?"

"Sit and talk."

"About what?"

"Anything you like. Occasionally *I'll* start the ball rolling, but in the main it's left to you."

"Group therapy," she commented. "Poor man's analysis!"

"Don't minimise the results it achieves." He went over to the sink and poured out the dregs of his tea. He rinsed the mug and then carefully refilled it from the teapot, using a strainer to trap the leaves. All his gestures were controlled, giving indication that he was a man used to looking after himself.

Not the sort to subsist on bread and jam if he were left

alone Nicola suddenly knew, and was annoyed with herself for having been sorry for him when he had first started to eat that ridiculous mixture of jam sandwich, pickle and ham.

"Have you ever had group therapy before?" he asked, returning to the table.

"Certainly not. Whatever gave you that idea?"

"Your comments on it were pretty pointed."

"I've read books."

"How old were you when you left school?"

"Eighteen," she answered without thinking, and seeing the disbelief in his eyes knew she had said the wrong thing. "Er – fifteen," she lied. "I – er – wasn't very clever."

"I wouldn't have said that."

"I've got *Reader's Digest* knowledge," she averred and, unwilling for him to question her further, decided to do the questioning herself. "Where did you get the money to start this place?"

"The house was given to me by the Council. I only had to furnish it. And find the rates each year," he added.

"What about the running expenses? They must be high."

"I manage," he said briefly.

"How?" she persisted.

"A few people help. I'd like more, but I manage."

"What good do you hope to do? I mean, what's the purpose of a place like this?"

"It's somewhere for people to come. A place where they can talk over their problems."

"Do you get crazy people too?"

"That word is meaningless. Every emotion that we can't control can become a craziness inside us. But when we see that craziness in perspective we can learn how to handle it."

"Have you helped many people since you started?"

"Enough to make it worthwhile." He leaned against the

sink. "I like to think I help all my patients in some degree or another."

"So we're your patients too? I'd have thought you'd like us to think of you as our friend or counsellor – or some such phoney euphemism." She was being deliberately rude, refusing to let herself be affected by his seriousness. She could not remember ever having such a serious conversation with any man she had known. Excepting Marty, of course, but he was like her father and couldn't be counted.

"Why are you on the defensive again?" Barnaby Grayson asked, putting his mug on the sink.

"I'm not," she snapped. "I just can't stand idealists."

"Neither can I. I'd shoot 'em all at thirty! After that age they tend to become fanatics."

"You don't mean that."

"I do," he assured her. "Work it out for yourself and I think you'll agree with me." He glanced at his watch, a large serviceable one, and pulled a face. "I'm late for the session." He moved to the door. "Coming?"

"Just like that?"

"It's open to everyone."

"I'll listen," she said, "but I won't join in."

He shrugged and went upstairs ahead of her, suddenly the doctor; no longer the man.

43

CHAPTER FOUR

Nicola's first day at the hostel had been so busy that it was evening before she realised it. True to her word she had sat in on the group discussion, held in what appeared to be a general common-room, and furnished with dilapidated sofas and easy chairs. Expecting a serious, quiet-spoken meeting, she had been astonished when it had turned into a general free-for-all, with several of the young men and women speaking at the same time and one boy of about eighteen storming out in a temper. His departure provoked a further discussion, though his return some few minutes later evoked no comment, and was accepted as a natural course of events.

Barnaby Grayson only spoke when the conversation reached a hiatus, and she noted that he always brought up a point that would lead to one or other of the group taking command, expounding their own thoughts which were then dissected by the rest. Sometimes the frankness was brutal, but it took little intelligence to see the therapeutic effect of such verbal cleansing, and though she held herself aloof from the discussion – as she had said she would – she could not help being deeply interested in it.

Having enjoyed a carefree life, untouched by problems, she was surprised by her reactions to this totally alien world in which she was now living. It made her realise how barren her own life was, and she felt regret that she had not taken her headmistress's advice and gone to university. But the thought of studying for studying's sake had not appealed to her, it had seemed pointless to learn a profession which she would have no necessity to practise, and to get a degree in the arts or social sciences merely for the sake of having it had been less appealing than throwing up her studies completely and travelling round the world with her godfather to see all the Rosten factories.

Unfortunately, on her return she had faced a blank future, and within six months the continuous round of pleasure-seeking had begun to pall, bringing with it a depression that could not be assuaged by buying new clothes or discovering a new restaurant for dinner.

Her meeting with Jeffrey and her subsequent engagement had led her to hope she had met someone who would at last give her life more meaning, but he had merely seen their future as a continuation of the present, blessed by the legality of a wedding ceremony and possibly children, but not being seriously affected by either.

More and more she had come to realise that one day she would have to make a decision about her life. But because she had been afraid where this would lead, she had fought against it, acting more gaily the more bored she became, becoming more extravagant the more guilty she felt by her wealth. Discovering Jeffrey in Deborah's arms had only been the spur to something which had already been formulating in her mind: a desire to change her life, to do something of value no matter how difficult the doing of it was. But not in her wildest imaginings had she thought to find herself in a haven for mixed-up youngsters of her own generation. Her idea of doing something worthwhile had veered towards making life pleasant for the impoverished gentility, providing television sets for the house-bound elderly or a beautifully equipped orphanage for talcum-sweet babies. She had certainly not seen herself taking an interest in girls who had left home at fifteen to become vagrants, or were so troubled by their emotional immaturity that the slightest problem created a trauma that shattered their ability to cope with life. Here was a rawness she had never anticipated and, even as it appalled and horrified her, it filled her with unexpected compassion.

As the young people around her unburdened their problems, she found it difficult to remain aloof, and she was glad when the session ended and she could disappear to the safety of the kitchen, where she tried to make a pretence of helping with the preparation of supper.

"You're a lousy bread-cutter," Carole said, taking the knife from her and surveying the inch-thick diagonal slices. "You're obviously used to buying it sliced."

"I rarely eat bread," Nicola replied.

"What do you fill up on – potatoes?"

It took a moment for Nicola to understand the meaning, and she nodded and turned away to get the cutlery, which seemed to be permanently kept in a heap on a tray. "Do we always eat in the kitchen?" she asked.

"There ain't no dining-room," a young man who had come down to slice the meat informed her.

Everybody went into gales of laughter and Nicola bit her lip. She should have realised a dining-room would be considered a waste of space when every available room was given over to accommodation.

"Don't mind us laughing at you." It was the lank-haired blonde girl – Gillian she called herself, but she had, it seemed, steadfastly refused to tell anyone her surname. "There isn't all that much to laugh at round here."

"You all seem very happy," Nicola commented.

"Don't let appearances fool you. This place is the land of limbo. You stay here for a while and pretend everything's going to be fine – except that you know that the minute you leave here the whole rotten world will come crashing down on your head again."

"Aren't you rather young to write the world off as rotten?"

"What's age got to do with it? Eldest of seven kids I was, with a mother who ran off and left us when I was ten. I soon got to know what the world was then."

"How awful for you!"

"No good harking back to the past," Carole intervened. "We *all* had a rough time."

"What happened to you when your mother left?" Nicola asked Gillian, too interested to change the subject.

"We were put in an orphanage. I ran away three times, and the last time they didn't catch me. Now I'm too old for them to take me back."

"How long have you been here?"

"Eight weeks. I never stay anywhere longer than that. If I do, things start closing in on me. That's when I pack up and run."

"So you'll be leaving soon?"

Gillian turned away. "Barnaby's on at me to stay. But I'm not sure."

"Perhaps he thinks he can help you."

"I don't want to be helped. I'm happy the way I am."

The serving of supper prevented further conversation and Nicola, anticipating seeing Barnaby Grayson, was disappointed to find that Joanna took his meal upstairs on a tray, together with her own.

"It's the only time she gets him to herself," Carole proclaimed. Of all the girls in the hostel she was the most vociferous, making loud comments on everything and everybody. Not that anyone took much notice of her – though this remark elicited several ribald ones.

"The only reason dear Joanna puts up with *us*," said a young man called Frank, "is because Barnaby puts up with *her*."

"She'll catch him one day," Gillian said.

"You talk as if he hasn't got a mind of his own," Nicola put in.

"He's got a mind," said Frank. "What he hasn't got is a life! And that's what Joanna's banking on. All work and no play is bound to give you the itch, sooner or later, and she'll be there to do the scratching!"

"That's not the story I've heard," Carole took up the conversation again. "The nurses in the hospital fall for him ten a penny."

Talk turned to the availability of women in general, and Nicola concentrated on her supper thinking longingly of what she might be eating if she were at home.

It was only when washing-up was completed – her second wet immersion of the day – that she wondered where she would be sleeping that night. She had not considered this aspect when she had decided to stay here for a week, and disturbed by the prospect of sharing a room with three other girls, she debated whether to go and find Barnaby Grayson and tell him she was leaving after all.

She was hovering uncertainly by the sink when he came in.

"I'll have to call you Cinderella," he said.

"Why?"

"I always find you in the kitchen!"

"You called me Cinderella last night too."

"That was because of your clothes."

"My haute couture dress, you mean," she smiled.

He seemed pleased that she could make a joke about her dress, when only yesterday she had been furious with him for commenting on it, and seeing him relax she hastily asked where she would be sleeping that night.

"Not in my room," he replied. "Once is permissible, twice

would be permissive!"

"I've no designs on you," she said coldly.

"Good." As always, her sarcasm had no effect. "I've fixed up for you to sleep with Gillian. It's a small room and on the top floor."

"Why didn't you suggest it last night?"

"It would have meant moving beds around and waking up the household." He came closer, looming tall and broad above her. "You look like a washed-out haddock."

"I'm not used to so much washing-up."

"Didn't you do any when you were a waitress?"

Too late she remembered her lie. If she spun her yarn any longer, she'd get tripped up by it! "I only carried trays," she said quickly. "Washing up was done by a machine. You could do with one here."

"We could do with a lot of things."

They were now in the upstairs hall and he motioned her to the sitting-room. "Make yourself comfortable. I'll be with you in a minute."

She glanced at the empty room and then over to the common-room where she could hear the sound of voices. Intercepting her glance, Barnaby shook his head. "I'd like to talk to you," he explained, and waited for her to move towards the sitting-room before disappearing round the back of the stairs.

On the threshold Nicola paused. It was imperative that she telephone her godfather. It had been impossible to leave the hostel during the day and equally impossible to use the telephone she had noticed in the office when she had gone there with Joanna. But now she was sure the office was empty, and she sped towards it. It was in darkness, and though reluctant to put on the light, she had to do so in order to dial. Hurriedly she did so, her heart beating more loudly than the ringing of the telephone. If only someone would answer it quickly before

Barnaby Grayson came in search of her! After what seemed an eternity the receiver was picked up and she heard her godfather's voice.

"Marty," she said. "It's me – Nicola."

"Good grief!" his voice boomed down the receiver. "Where on earth have you been? I was giving you till midnight. If you hadn't shown up by then I was going to call the police."

"Thank heavens you didn't. I'm perfectly safe."

"Where are you?"

"In a hostel."

"Be serious, Nicola," he begged.

"I am."

Quickly she told him of the events that had brought her here.

"I'm glad you found out about Jeffrey," Marty commented gruffly. "I know it hurts, but you'll get over it. Now give me your address and I'll send a car for you."

Reluctantly she told him where she was. "But I'm not coming home yet," she repeated. "And you're not to come after me."

"Why not? You're not in any trouble, are you?"

"No, but I might create a bit!"

"Don't do anything foolish, Nicola. Remember who you are."

"They don't know it here."

"What does that mean?"

From the corner of her eye she saw Barnaby Grayson come out of his bedroom. What a fool she had been not to remember that his room was directly opposite the office. He could now hear every word she said. She pressed the phone closer to her ear. "Don't come after me," she said yet again.

"I don't like it, Nicola. It's dangerous for you to be wandering around alone."

"I'm in no more danger than I was with you," she said, and saw Barnaby stiffen.

"Now look here," her godfather said tersely, "you're too old to go acting so irresponsibly. I'll come and fetch you myself."

"Leave me alone, Marty. I'm not coming back!"

There was a momentary silence and she could hear her godfather breathing heavily.

"Will you call me again soon, Nicola?"

"Yes. Goodbye." She put down the telephone, aware of the man in the doorway. "Do you always listen to other people's conversations?" she asked.

"Only if I can't avoid it. I assume it was the boy-friend?" He went on before she could reply, "I'm glad you were firm about not going back to him."

"I was very firm," she said. "He isn't good for me."

"I agree with *that*," Barnaby retorted crisply. "A man who can let you go around the way you –"

"I left all the clothes he bought me," she interrupted. "When I left him it didn't seem right to take them."

He gave a grunt. "Now you've made your call we can have our chat."

"I don't intend regaling you with the history of my life."

"I'm sure you'll find something to talk about." She tossed her head and he gave a warm chuckle and slipped his arm across her shoulders. "I keep forgetting what a little thing you are. I suppose it's because you've got such a long tongue!"

"You're not so bad at talking yourself."

"It's my job," he commented.

But when they were both in the sitting room he made no effort to question her, nor even to speak, and Nicola – tired from a day of unaccustomed work – found it difficult to keep her eyes open. Not even the thought of having to share a room with Gillian could detract from the pleasure of being able to

51

rest her aching limbs. She must have washed and dried a couple of hundred dishes today, and ironed at least a dozen sheets. Not bad going for a girl who had never done either before.

She yawned and tried to hide it, but not before the man saw it and smiled.

"You look exhausted. We'd better postpone our chat for another night."

She stood up before he could change his mind. Though she would have liked to talk to him she was too tired to do so. Besides, he was so astute that she would need all her wits about her when she did.

"Aren't you going to bed, too?" she asked.

"I've some notes to write up first." He sighed without realising it. "It's a good two-hour job."

"Can't you dictate it to your secretary?"

"I only have one in the hospital and it's more than I dare do to use her for my work here. And don't ask why I haven't got one here as well, because the answer should be obvious to you."

"Money," she said promptly.

"You catch on quick!" He grinned and, wishing her goodnight, went down the hall.

Slowly Nicola made her way to the top of the house. It grew progressively colder with each floor she mounted and she was shivering, despite her sweater, when she entered the room she was to share with Gillian. It was furnished with the bare necessities – two narrow beds, a strip of rug between them and a central bedside table for them to share. She was glad to see Gillian already asleep, and she hurriedly undressed and climbed into bed. It was a far cry from the posture-sprung luxury of her Belgravia one, but she was too tired to care, and hardly had her head touched the pillow when she fell fast asleep.

Wintery sunlight, shining full into her eyes through the uncurtained attic window, woke her up to another day, and she was shivering as she pulled the blanket more closely around her and thought how staggered Marty would be if he could see her now, sleeping in her petticoat on a lumpy divan. If she was going to stay here the week as she had planned, she would have to get a change of clothing and a nightdress.

Her second day was almost a replica of her first. There did not seem to be any set rules and everyone was free to come and go as they liked, providing they put in an appearance at the discussion group which was held either in the afternoon or evening, depending when Barnaby was free.

Listening to the way everyone spoke about him, she realised how highly he was regarded. He was not thought of as a doctor looking down on them from some lofty pedestal, or an intellectual working out his own particular problems by trying to work out theirs. Rather he was seen as being their equal, with a deep understanding that made him able to appreciate other people's troubles without condemning them or even advising, unless he was asked to do so.

It was this lack of advice, this determination to proffer no counsel unless it was sought, which seemed to be his greatest asset. And hearing Gillian and Carole, as well as several of the young men, refer to it, she wondered why he had been so quick to give both his opinions and his counsel to *her*. Was it because of a subconscious recognition that she was different, or because she had shown more defiance than anyone else?

Joanna was far less liked than Barnaby, and though accepted by the dozen or so young men, was barely tolerated by the girls. Nicola could not believe that Barnaby was unaware of the lack of empathy that existed between Joanna and the occupants of the hostel, and surmised he was in no position financially to turn down anyone who offered to help him run his project. The question was whether Joanna would be successful in running Barnaby!

Nicola was pondering on whether or not Joanna would remain at the hostel if she did not achieve her ambition, when the object of her thoughts walked in carrying a bulging linen sack.

"Clothes from the cleaners," Joanna said. "Would you give me a hand with them?"

Nicola complied, helping the girl tip the things on to the kitchen table. There was a preponderance of jeans and sweaters, with several threadbare coats and jackets. Rummaging through them, she found her dress, hiding a smile as she saw its clean but wispy tatters.

"This is yours too, I believe." Joanna held out Nicola's fur. No longer flattened by damp and stained with mud, each pelt was luxuriantly thick and glistened like satin.

Nicola went to take hold of the fur, but Joanna stepped back, still firmly clutching it.

"It looks quite different now it's cleaned. If I had realised what fur it was I wouldn't have sent it to be machine-washed!"

"I think it's come up very well," Nicola said casually, and put her hand on it.

But Joanna still held it firmly. "Even so, one doesn't normally send mink to the dry-cleaners."

Nicola could not prevent the colour rushing into her cheeks, and seeing it, Joanna gave an unpleasant smile.

"Where did *you* get a fur like this?"

"I bought it."

"Pull the other one!"

"It's true. I didn't steal it, if that's what you're implying. I bought it."

"What did you use for money?"

"It's none of your business!"

"Everything you do while you're here is our business, Nicky, and if you stole this mink then you're liable to go to prison."

Nicola thought quickly. This was a situation she had not anticipated, and for the first time her nimble brain could not find an excuse to get her out of trouble. She could not let Joanna think she was a thief, yet equally she could not tell her the truth. There must be something she could say to explain how she had come to be in possession of the mink.

"I was —" she began, and then stopped as Barnaby Grayson came in.

"Coming to the discussion, Nicky?" he asked.

"Yes," she said quickly, and went to hurry past him, but Joanna stepped to one side and barred her way.

"You're not going yet. I want to get to the bottom of this first."

"Bottom of what?" Barnaby enquired.

"Nothing," Nicola mumbled, but was interrupted by Joanna who held out the mink stole.

"Nicky was wearing this when Mrs. Thomas brought her here. I had it cleaned with her dress."

"So what?" Barnaby shrugged.

"It's mink," Joanna explained irritably. "It's quite obvious Nicky stole it."

"I didn't steal it," Nicola said hotly. "You've no right to call me a thief!"

"Then why won't you tell me where you got it? Or do you seriously expect me to believe it's part of your wardrobe?"

"Joanna — let me handle this." Barnaby was no longer
55

placid, and there was a serrated edge to his voice.

Dropping the fur on the table, Joanna walked out, and Barnaby leaned against the wall and looked at Nicola.

She waited for him to speak, but the seconds passed and she knew he intended her to do so first.

"I didn't steal it," she repeated. "I – I – found it."

"In your Christmas stocking?"

"Don't be funny," she replied haughtily. "I wouldn't expect you to believe *that*."

"Yet you expect me to believe you *found* it!"

"Yes. I was a waitress – you already know that – and one of the customers went out and left it on her chair. It was a discothèque," she added quickly. "One of those dark noisy rooms – you know the sort of place I mean."

He nodded but did not answer, and she knew he was waiting for her to continue.

"I suppose I should have run after her with it, but I – it was too much of a temptation. I've never had a fur before, never even possessed a piece of rabbit skin." Nicola made herself look forlorn, drooping her shoulders and letting her hands hang limply at her sides. "When I picked up that mink I just couldn't give it back. I *had* to keep it – even if only for a night."

"When did you intend to return it?"

"I was going to do so the night that Mrs. Thomas knocked me down." She looked him fully in the face, making her eyes as large and guileless as she could. "I didn't intend to keep it. You've got to believe me."

She went on staring at him, all at once feeling it was terribly important that he did. Breathlessly she waited for his reply, and when it came – a mere nod of his head – she felt an inexplicable surge of pleasure.

"As you intended sending it back," he murmured, "I assume you know to whom it belongs?"

"Of course. The girl was a regular customer."

"You'd better give me the address and I'll see it's returned today. I'd better explain how you came to have it – that you were on your way to return it when you were knocked down."

"There's no need for you to take it. I'll do it myself."

The look that flashed into his eyes told her she had said the wrong thing, and hastily she back-tracked. "It isn't that I don't want you to return it – it's just that it's an imposition to bother with it."

"It would be more of a bother if the police came looking for you."

"Can't we send it through the post? That way you wouldn't have to answer any questions."

He rubbed a hand through his hair, and she noticed that though it was thick, it was very fine and soft. "There's no reason why we can't post it, I suppose. As you say, it will save explanations."

He took a notebook from his pocket and looked at her. Keeping her voice expressionless she gave him her own surname and address, deliberately omitting the Christian name in case it struck him as being too similar to her own.

"Rosten," he muttered. "Isn't that the cereal heiress?"

Not trusting herself to speak, she nodded.

"Someone like that makes my shackles rise." He slipped the notebook back into his pocket. "I don't see how anyone can morally justify having so much money."

"She probably inherited it."

"Makes no difference. It's hers now."

"Do you think she should give it away?"

"I would if it were me."

"Spend it on houses like this, I suppose?"

"Or other projects. I certainly wouldn't let it lie in the bank multiplying itself like a cancer."

"What a cruel thing to say!" Nicola could not keep the tremble of anger from her voice. "That money gives employment to thousands of people. It isn't just left in the bank – it's invested in factories and equipment – and lots of other things, I suppose," she concluded hurriedly.

"I didn't think you were the type to defend the bloated rich." Barnaby Grayson looked definitely amused.

"I didn't think you were the type to condemn them out of hand," she said hotly.

"It seems we don't know each other very well."

"Are you a Communist?" she accused.

For a split second he looked astonished, then his mouth widened in a grin, showing his white teeth. "I'm a dyed-in-the-wool capitalist, Nicky. I've got this beautiful house and my aim is to have as many more as I can!"

"Only because you want to turn them into shelters," she said with a toss of her head. "That isn't answering my question at all."

"I didn't think it worth answering. I believe in the freedom of the individual, and that precludes a police state." His grin became wider. "Does that answer your question?"

She nodded and he went to the door, still holding the fur.

"You aren't going to deliver it to the house yourself, are you?" she asked impulsively.

"We'd already decided I wouldn't do that. I'll insure it and send it through the post."

Later that night, as she thought about her scene with Barnaby, Nicola wondered whether he really believed she had intended to return the mink. If she had been in his position she certainly wouldn't have done so; but then women were generally more suspicious than men, and unlikely to give their own sex the benefit of the doubt: as Joanna had clearly shown.

Nicola frowned. What *was* there about Joanna Morgan that set her teeth on edge? Surely it was more than just her bossy manner and proprietorial attitude towards Barnaby Grayson? It was amazing the way he didn't appear to mind it, or perhaps habit had dulled his perception. There was no denying she would make him an excellent wife, able to share his private, as well as his working life.

"Fat lot of private life he's got," she said aloud, thinking of the evening that had just passed, with Barnaby sharing his sitting room with a dozen youngsters all vying for his attention. Yet despite it, he had tried to single out Nicky to talk to, and it had required all her adroitness to avoid him. But sooner or later he would expect to hear the full story of her life. She half smiled, and pulled the blanket around her. She must be ready to hand him a good one. Then, when he had swallowed it, she would tell him the truth. The anticipation of doing so was becoming more and more pleasant.

CHAPTER FIVE

Nicola's opportunity to talk to Barnaby Grayson alone came the following morning.

Gillian had been restless during the night – a nightmare, she had explained apologetically, when her sudden sharp cries had woken Nicola up at three o'clock in the morning – and Nicola had taken a long time to fall asleep again, still unused to her hard-sprung bed, so that the morning sun failed in its usual task of waking her up and, hearing Gillian noisily dress and go downstairs, had mumbled that she would follow in a minute, and then promptly fallen asleep again.

It was considerably later when she sped down to the kitchen. The steamy air was already full of the smell of cooking vegetables, and abandoning all thought of breakfast, she went over to take out the ironing board.

"You'd better leave that," Carole Stritch called out. "Barnaby left word he wants to see you."

Nicola jumped guiltily. "How long has he been waiting?"

"Does it matter? He's not your boss."

Acknowledging the truth of this, she hurried upstairs to the sitting room.

He was at the table writing, but looked up and smiled as she came in. "Had a good sleep?"

She flushed. "I'm sorry I'm late, but I –"

"Why do you always think I'm criticising you," he interrupted. "I'm not running a boarding-school. You're free to get up any time you like." He beckoned her forward. "Come and sit by the fire. You look frozen."

"You keep the house too cold."

"I'm lucky to keep it at all!"

Annoyed at her runaway tongue she said: "Why do you want to see me?"

"For our chat – or were you hoping I'd forgotten?"

He came over and sat in an easy chair opposite her. He looked relaxed and pleased with himself. The benign psychologist, she thought crossly, all ready to sort out the problems of a mixed-up girl. Well, she intended to make herself as mixed-up as a bowl of spaghetti.

"What would you like to know, Dr. Grayson?"

"Like that, eh?" he said, raising his brows in mock surprise. "We *are* formal today."

"You're a doctor. Why pretend you're not?"

"I don't pretend. I just prefer to be called Barnaby."

"Even in your hospital?"

"Unfortunately I have to be called Doctor there, but that's because it isn't *my* hospital."

"I'm sure you'll end up having one of your own," she said, with mock innocence. "If you could marry an heiress –"

"And exchange one prison for another?" He grinned and shook his head. "We're supposed to be talking about *your* life, Nicky."

"I don't see why we should." She gave him the full battery of her eyes. "Let's keep my life private."

"It would have been pretty public if you hadn't been brought here."

"What do you mean?"

"It's obvious." He leaned forward, his rough wool sweater strained by his broad shoulders. "You've got no fixed address – at least none you're willing to give us, and when Mrs. Thomas knocked you down you were wandering along the Embankment. My bet is that you were going to sleep rough."

His words gave her the lead she was looking for. "I was

running away. I'd decided to make a new life for myself."

"On the Embankment?"

"It was a starting place."

"A rather primitive one," he said whimsically. "Where was your original start?"

"In an orphanage," she said promptly. "It was a horrible place and I was always hungry."

"With a ghastly matron?"

"Ghastly," she agreed.

"When did you leave it?"

"I ran away when I was sixteen and came to London. I've been here ever since."

"Working as a ladies' maid and a waitress."

"I had other jobs too."

"Where did you meet Marty?"

"He's not important," she said hastily.

"But you were running away from him." Barnaby Grayson's voice was deceptively mild. "And he's still trying to get you back. Don't forget I heard you talking to him."

Looking at the steady grey eyes watching her, Nicola knew she would have to think fast. "He loves me. That's why he wants me back."

"Do you love him?"

"I'm very fond of him."

"How old is he?"

"Sixty," she said, and too late tried to draw the words back. "But he's very young for his age."

"He'd need to be!" Barnaby looked unexpectedly severe. "Isn't he rather old for a girl like you?"

"I'm not a child – even though I look it in these shapeless clothes."

"I know your shape," he reminded her. "You slept in my room, remember?"

Embarrassed, she averted her head. It was strange that Jeffrey's most blatant innuendoes had not affected her the way Barnaby's gentle teasing did.

"Did you live with Marty?" he persisted.

"Yes," she said, remembering the happy years of her childhood.

"Was *he* the person you were running away from when Mrs. Thomas found you?"

"Yes. I'd – I'd decided he *was* too old for me and I was going to make a new life for myself."

"With the mink?"

She blinked, then slowly nodded. Barnaby studied her thoughtfully, and only as his eyes narrowed did she realise she had said the wrong thing.

"If this Marty gave you the fur, why did you give me that address in Belgravia? It *was* the Rosten house – I looked it up in the telephone directory."

Nicola moistened her lips, unsure what to say. "I – er –" she floundered.

"Don't for heaven's sake tell me Marty lives there!" he exploded. "There's a limit even to *my* credulity!"

Since there was only a straw to clutch at, she did so. "He *does* live there," she asserted. "He's the butler."

Barnaby's jaw fell, and it was all she could do not to laugh.

"That's where I met him," she went on, warming to her subject. "I told you I was a ladies' maid and –"

"You mean that part of your story's true?"

"Of course. I was very close to Miss Rosten. I only left because I didn't want to see Marty. I couldn't expect *him* to change his job. After all, he's been with the family for years."

"So you left instead?"

"Yes."

He sighed. "You needn't have lied about where you got the

63

mink. I'm not here to judge you, Nicky. I'm here to help."

"You are helping," she said earnestly. "I sent the mink back to him, didn't I? At least *that's* a step in the right direction."

"Yes," he said briskly, "it is." He came to stand beside her. "I'm glad you left Miss Rosten. Acting as wet-nurse to a spoiled heiress isn't the job for you."

"That's what Marty said. He was always telling me I could do better."

"What did he mean?" Barnaby's voice was sharp and her hackles rose.

"Not *that*," she said frigidly.

"I'm glad to hear it. From the way you were talking to him the other night I got the impression he saw you as a meal ticket."

The thought of her meticulous godfather as a butler trying to set her up as a demi-mondaine brought a smile to her lips.

"I'm glad you find my remark amusing," Barnaby went on.

"Only because it's so ridiculous. Marty doesn't need *me* to keep him. He's a rich old dear — for a butler, I mean," she amended hastily.

"I suppose there are good pickings in the Rosten household."

"Excellent. Miss Rosten never has left-overs served up again, and she has a fresh bottle of wine with every meal."

"Champagne for breakfast, too, I don't doubt."

"Of course. She even washes her teeth in it!"

He laughed. "I won't swallow *that*. And I'm sure she doesn't either!"

Nicola smiled. "As a matter of fact, she's awfully nice."

He grunted and turned away, busying himself with the coal fire that burned half-heartedly in the grate.

Nicola studied him as he raked the ashes and put on more

64

coal. Not good-looking in the accepted sense – his features were too irregular for that – he exuded a powerful and virile masculinity despite the fact that he made no concession to his appearance. When he had returned from the hospital she had noticed that his suit, though dark and conservative, had seen better days. Now, in slacks and sweater – which seemed to be a second skin to him – he looked more equipped for the rugger field than for dealing with today's disturbed generation.

As though aware of her gaze, he ran a hand through his hair in an attempt to smooth it, but though he pulled it away from his forehead, a thick strand fell forward again immediately, and lay soft and silky above his deep-set grey eyes.

"What's *your* background?" she asked with forced casualness.

"I was born and educated in Birmingham and came to London to do post-graduate work. I've been here ever since."

"Were you always interested in helping people?"

"I suppose so. It wasn't until I was left a small legacy a couple of years ago that I was able to do anything about it."

"I thought you said the Council gave you this house?"

"They did. But it had to be furnished, and there's rates and heating and food to buy each week. Thirty-odd people take a lot of feeding."

"Can't you get a grant from the Council?"

"Not unless I let them have a say in the way this place is run. And I prefer to do it *my* way."

"Backing your own opinion?"

"I won't be the first person to have done so."

She remembered her grandfather who had begun the family fortune in a similar way, practically selling his wife and children in order to raise the money to make and package cereals in his own particular method. But somehow she could not see

Barnaby achieving the same fame and fortune. Fame, perhaps, she decided, looking at his strong face, but never the money he would need to put his plans into action.

"You need a rich benefactor," she stated, and then added provokingly: "You're so good-looking, I'm sure you could find one. Miss Rosten, for example."

Barnaby's expletive would not have received approval in august medical circles, and she lowered her lids to hide the mischief in her eyes.

"The one thing I *don't* want," he said forcefully, "is to be regarded as someone's pet charity! I've seen it happen to friends of mine. You end up nothing better than a paid lackey." He flung his arms wide. "Don't minimise what I've done here, Nicky. In the short time we've been going, this place has been home to more than a hundred people."

"Will I be hundred and one on your list of reformed characters?"

"Do you *need* reforming?" he asked gravely.

"*You* seem to think so."

"A mink doesn't make you a minx!"

She gave an exclamation and jumped up, not realising he was standing so close to her until the top of her head brushed against his chin. He stepped back quickly, but for an instant their gazes locked, hazel eyes staring into grey ones until she swung to the door.

"I'd better get back to my ironing."

"We'll talk some more another time," he replied, and returned to his papers by the table.

She glanced at him quickly, but he was already immersed, and realising he had forgotten her, she went out, feeling unexpectedly dejected.

Downstairs in the kitchen she found a mound of linen waiting to be ironed – it seemed to have mushroomed like fungi during the night – and despondently started dampening them and folding them up.

"Leave the sheets and give us a hand with the veg," Carole piped up. "Otherwise we'll be here all day!"

With alacrity Nicola put away the washing and picked up a knife. She had never before peeled potatoes, and she found it far more difficult than she could have believed possible. Thick lumps of peel and vegetable came away beneath her fingers, and the little knobbly chunks left bore no relation to the large brown potatoes in the sink.

"If you intend throwing away the potatoes and eating the peel," Carole said finally, "you're doing a grand job."

"I've never peeled potatoes before," Nicola explained.

"What did you eat then – crisps?"

"Cabbage and carrots," she said quickly.

"They need peeling too." Carole shook her head in exasperation. "Make a pot of tea instead. I'm gasping. You can take one up to Barnaby too."

Nicola put on the kettle, got out the cups and found an old brown tray for Barnaby, rummaging in a drawer until she found a coloured knapkin with which to cover the scuffed surface.

All the while Carole muttered to herself about the difficulties of preparing food in such a badly equipped kitchen, and how much better she would feel once she had packed her things and moved on. She was in one of her rumbustious moods which, according to Gillian, occurred at least twice a week.

"I know Barnaby would like Carole to stay here much longer," Gillian had confided to Nicola last night. "There's some reason why she hates staying anywhere for more than a month, and he's sure he can get to the bottom of it if he can talk to her long enough."

Nicola had been surprised by the warmth in which Gillian had spoken about Barnaby and recognising it, Gillian had looked half-defiant. "Most of the girls get a crush on him," she admitted, "but he never seems to notice. He treats everyone of us the same and —"

"He's a doctor," Nicola reminded her.

"I can tell you a few tales about doctors," Gillian had said, and had then proceeded to do so, concluding with the comment that Barnaby, of course, was quite different.

Remembering this conversation as she waited for the kettle to boil, Nicola marvelled that Barnaby could control such a motley collection as the group living here. It spoke well not only for his ability, but for his sympathy too. Somehow it no longer seemed so amusing to be able to confront him with her true identity. To begin with she had imagined he would be furious at being made a fool of, but now she had a feeling that he would take the whole thing in his stride, and would probably consider that *she* was the one who had been belittled; possibly even pitying her because she had found it necessary to play such a childish trick.

And it was childish, she admitted to herself, as she warmed the teapot and added the tea. Barnaby was an idealistic fool wasting his undoubted ability in this semi-derelict hostel when, if he had half an ounce of ambition, he'd be concentrating on becoming a senior consultant at his hospital. Yet he enjoyed the work he was doing here, she thought crossly as she poured milk into the cups. Even worse — he had every intention of continuing with it.

"I'll take the tray if you like," Gillian offered.

"It's no problem," Nicola replied, and though she would have liked to put her own cup of tea beside Barnaby's, she decided it would be too obvious. But perhaps he would talk to her while he was eating. She might even tell him the truth about herself now.

Carefully she mounted the stairs, anxious not to let the tea slop into the saucer. So careful were her movements that she was able to hear Barnaby talking in the sitting room before she even arrived at the door, and she saw that it was ajar.

"I don't know why you give so much time to Nicky Rose," Joanna was saying.

"I don't," Barnaby replied. "I've only had one proper talk with her since she arrived."

"Why bother at all? There's nothing wrong with her."

"I'm not so sure. You should have heard the story she spun me this morning. Bleak orphanage, not enough food, a matron who was little better than a witch, and escape to the bright lights of London when she was sixteen."

"That seems quite feasible," Joanna said somewhat doubt-fully.

"You just have to look at the girl to know it isn't true." There was exasperation in Barnaby's voice. "Her whole be-haviour – the way she talks and moves – shows a good cultural background and education – far better than she'd get in an orphanage. Personally I'd say she comes from a middle-class home and ran away in search of excitement."

"What about the mink and the aged boy-friend?"

"That part sounds true." Barnaby's voice was serious. "She wouldn't be the first girl to fall for the lure of a fur and a few fancy trimmings!"

"I should imagine she knew very well where it was lead-ing," came Joanna's cold tones. "Girls of her type fall for the mink and diamond syndrome."

Nicola drew a furious breath. Anger with Barnaby for dis-believing her carefully fabricated story was only partially mol-lified by hearing his defence of her. Though he considered her a highly imaginative liar he didn't – unlike Joanna – consider her beyond redemption.

Cheeks stained red, she kicked open the door with her foot and marched in.

"Tea – just what I needed," Barnaby remarked, coming over to the table as she set down the tray. "Bring up a cup for yourself and join us."

"I've work to do."

"You sound very hard done by," Joanna said in dulcet tones. "What are you doing?"

"Polishing my diamonds," Nicola said with sarcastic sweetness, and ran out, but not before she heard Barnaby's shout of laughter.

Drat the man! He didn't even have the decency to be embarrassed at knowing she had overheard their conversation. He was thick-skinned and insufferable and smugly certain he could read her like a book. Well, he was in for a surprise when he discovered that the cover she presented to *him* in no way gave indication of the content of the pages.

CHAPTER SIX

Anger against Barnaby made Nicola revise her plans. The momentary feeling of warmth she had had for him had been dispelled by hearing his conversation with Joanna, and what had begun as a light-hearted deception now held a far deeper significance. She would stay here one week not only to show him how easily he could be fooled, but also how sadly he could misjudge character.

During the next few days she went out of her way to confuse him, and was pliable one moment and rounding on him like a spitfire the next. Like everyone else in the hostel she attended his daily sessions and racked her brains each night to present him with a different problem each day.

Soon it became a battle of wits between them, and though she was sure he did not believe the problems she posed to him each day, he allowed them to go unchallenged.

On the morning of the seventh day Nicola awakened before Gillian and, staring through the small window at the dingy rooftops, wondered why she should feel so depressed. Today of all days she should be happy, for this was the moment she had been dreaming of: the day she was going to tell Barnaby her true identity.

Racing down the corridor to commandeer the bathroom, she hastily washed in tepid water and combed her hair in front of the fly-blown mirror. A week of comparatively early nights – without Jeffrey to keep her dancing till three in the morning – had given her skin a bloom it had not had for several years. Her eyes were brighter too, more green than hazel now that they were rested, and her hair, free of stylised settings, hung straight and silky around her shoulders. Not a suitable style for the scene ahead of her, she decided, and tied it back from her face with a narrow piece of ribbon. The simple style suited her delicately-cut features, and minus her usual layer of make-up she could have passed for a teenager. Remembering her usual daily performance with body lotion, face lotion, moisturising creams and powders, she marvelled that she looked none the worse without them – better, in fact. She only regretted her lack of mascara, and looked critically at her long, curling lashes.

"Hurry up in there!" someone shouted, banging on the bathroom door, and gathering up her flannel and towel she left the bathroom to someone else.

Returning to the bedroom she was surprised to see a small heap of clothing on her bed, and looked questioningly at Gillian who, having battled unsuccessfully against a cold for the last few days, had been ordered not to leave her room.

"Barnaby brought them up," she croaked. "He came in to have a look at me and left them."

Nicola lifted up a soft green wool dress and a heather blue skirt with a matching jumper. Even without trying them on she knew they would be a considerably better fit than what she had been wearing. The clothes were obviously new and she frowned, puzzled to know where he had got them. Still, people often gave away clothes they had never worn, and he obviously had a good source.

She put on the jumper and skirt and felt considerably more civilised now that she no longer looked so shapeless.

"And you look older in those," Gillian commented.

"Only because they give me more shape."

"They do more than give you shape," the girl coughed. "They accentuate the positive!"

Nicola peered at herself in the small mirror that hung on

the back of the door. "The sweater's a bit tight," she agreed.

"The boys will like it."

"Blow the boys!" Nicola waved at Gillian and went downstairs, anticipating and receiving appreciative whistles as she entered the kitchen.

However, her depression did not lift, and it coloured the morning, slowing down her actions and responses. She tried to make herself feel better by envisaging her forthcoming meeting with Barnaby. Should she waylay him this afternoon before he began the usual therapeutic discussion, or should she wait till it was over and he was relaxed before dinner? Or perhaps after dinner would be better. Yet if she left it so late she would have to remain here the entire day, and she had planned to return home for dinner – a dinner which she would thankfully have had no hand in preparing. What pleasure it would be to sit at her own elegant Regency table and eat food concocted by a master chef.

She closed her eyes the better to savour the thought, but it was too ephemeral to overcome the present odour of beef stew and cabbage. This acknowledgment brought forth another reason for her depression. How could she expect herself to be pleased at the thought of returning to the quiet loneliness of Belgravia when the rumbustious life – warm with comradeship and bristling with discussion and argument – was still going on so strongly around her? Not until she was far away from here and once more accustomed to cosseting and luxury would her spirits return to normal.

At mid-morning Joanna unexpectedly called her into the office. As usual the girl's behaviour could not be faulted. She was politely interested in all Nicola was doing, yet managed to give the impression that she did not like her. None of the other girls had mentioned that Joanna had ever been antagonistic towards them, and Nicola wondered why she herself had aroused it; had in fact felt it strongly almost from their first meeting.

"You've been here a week," Joanna was saying purposefully, "and it's usual for girls who can do so to try and find a job."

"I'm doing the ironing and dish-washing."

"I meant earning money."

"Are you asking me to leave the hostel?"

"No," Joanna said in a tone that suggested she did. "But unless someone is very disturbed emotionally we feel it's better for them to have a regular occupation. Even if it's only part-time."

"Is this Barnaby's order?"

"I haven't discussed it with *Doctor* Grayson. He generally leaves this sort of thing to me."

"I'd still like to talk to *Barnaby* about it." Nicola stressed his name deliberately and saw Joanna flush. "I intended talking to him today anyway."

"You take up enough of his time already," Joanna commented sharply. "He has far more important things to do than worry about *you*."

The attack was so uncalled-for that Nicola had to use all her self-control not to answer back. Since she could not find any logical reason for it, only an illogical one came to mind: Joanna was jealous of her. She turned in her chair and looked full into Joanna's face, seeing the thick white skin that so successfully masked her feelings, and the hard brown eyes that gazed at her with cool indifference. "I bet she was head girl at her school," Nicola thought, but kept her own features as composed as the ones opposite her.

"I've a list of jobs I think you might find suitable," Joanna said. "None of them are far from here, so you wouldn't be involved in any travelling expenses. A part-time salesgirl is wanted in a wool shop; a solicitor's office needs a telephonist – it's only a small switchboard so it shouldn't be difficult – and –"

"No job as a waitress?" Nicola asked brightly.

"Doctor Grayson wouldn't approve of that."

"I thought you hadn't discussed it with him."

"I know what his thoughts are on the subject," Joanna replied, "and for the time being he feels it would be better if you were in a job where you wouldn't have any temptation to revert to – to become – you know what I mean."

"You're making darn sure I do!" Nicola said angrily. "Keep your jobs, *Miss* Morgan. I don't need *you* to find me one!"

"If you intend staying here –"

"I don't!" Nicola retorted, and swung out of the room, colliding against a broad, white-shirted chest. With a gasp she looked up – a long way up – into Barnaby Grayson's face. "You've been eavesdropping," she accused.

"It's a habit I learned from you!" As always he refused to be provoked. "Actually I was on my way to see Joanna when I heard your – er – discussion. I was all set to intervene if a storm blew up." He looked at her quizzically. "You're not very diplomatic, are you, little Nicky?"

"Stop talking to me as if I'm a child!" She stepped back from him, unaware of her sweater outlined against the dark panelling of the wall, until she saw his eyes lower quickly and then rise to meet her own.

"You're certainly *not* a child," he said drily.

She reddened. "I – I want to thank you for the clothes."

"I'm glad to see they almost fit!" He folded his arms on his chest. "I gather you want to talk to me." Then seeing her questioning look: "I heard you tell Joanna."

"We can leave it till later," she stammered.

"There's no time like the present. Come into the sitting room now."

He caught her arm and pulled her forward, and her skin tingled at the pressure of his fingers. Aware of him in a way she had never been before, she pretended to a nonchalance she did not feel and moved away from him as soon as they entered the room.

Perhaps the knowledge that she would soon be disclosing her real identity and showing him how easily he had been duped was making her see him more as a man, and not as a doctor and the guiding light of this hostel? Yet it had been her antagonism towards him as a man – her resentment of his superior male belief that he knew everything better than she did – which had first decided her to maintain her charade with him. It was strange to think that the very characteristic which she had disliked in him then she now found disturbingly attractive.

Annoyed by her feelings, she tried to rationalise them away. She had been absent from her friends too long; she was missing Jeffrey and needed the assurance that she was still a desirable female. Yet even when she had felt herself to be desired she had never known – in her innermost heart – how much of her attraction was her own and how much her money.

"You look as though you're thinking sombre thoughts," Barnaby Grayson's deep voice interrupted her reverie, and with a start she raised her head to his.

His gaze was as penetrating as it always was and just as kind. There was no need to ask herself how he saw her: he made it all too clear that she was a girl in need of a strong, guiding hand to keep her on the path of virtue. Yet he saw her as a person of some sensitivity too. This much was obvious from the way in which – understanding her dislike of Joanna – he had brought her in here to try and placate her. But how quickly the kindly look on his face would disappear when he learned whom she was. She would tell him now, she decided, but even though she parted her lips, no words emerged.

"Well," he said encouragingly, "what do you want to tell me?"

"It wasn't important," she hedged, and lowered her eyes to the carpet. She raised them again and saw him stifle a yawn. "If I'm boring you," she said angrily, "I'll go."

"Don't be silly. I'm just tired."

He stifled another yawn and for the first time she noticed his pallor and red-rimmed eyes. "You shouldn't work so hard," she burst out, her anger dissolving. "People don't appreciate it. What with the hospital and this hostel you'll be an old man at forty."

"Old but happy!"

Tenderness tugged at her, and the urge to put her arms around him was so strong that she took a step forward. Her foot caught on a bare patch of carpet and the faint pull of the threads was enough to pull her back to her senses.

What was this crazy thing that was happening to her? No man had ever provoked her to such tenderness. Men were strong and had to be fought against, or were weak and were to be despised. But this man had no weakness for her to despise, nor did she want to fight his strength.

"What's the matter?" he asked.

"You're the matter," she snapped. "You look tired and old."

"You said you like older men!" He was still teasing. "I'd be a much better counsellor for you than Marty."

Anger rose in her again and she turned her back on him. A floorboard creaked and he stopped directly behind her, his hand coming down to her shoulder, the rounded bone fitting into the curve of his palm.

"Don't be annoyed with me for teasing you, Nicky."

"Why do you do it? You never tease the others."

"Perhaps you're a special case."

Intensely aware of his touch, she tried to keep her voice casual. "I bet you say that to all your patients."

"I don't regard you as a patient," he said, and dropped his hand.

"Why not?" She half glanced at him. "Don't you think I need your help?"

"Not in the way the other girls do."

Her heart began to thump, but she remained silent, and after a slight pause, he continued.

"From the moment you came here, you put on an act. Your story about the orphanage, for example. It just won't wash."

"Do you think I was lying about Marty too?" she said deliberately.

"I believe you were running away from a man," he replied, "and I believe your past life was extremely unhappy."

"Past life? You make it sound as if I came from another world!"

"I believe you do. And I also think you don't want to return to it. You haven't yet made up your mind *what* you want to do with your future, Nicky, and until you have, I'd like you to stay here."

She took back everything she had ever thought about his lack of perception. He had no way of knowing her identity, yet training and instinct had told him she was far different from what she appeared to be.

"If you do decide to stay on," he continued, "there's no need to come to the discussion groups if you don't want to. And I'll also tell Joanna to leave you alone."

"You mean I'm here as a non-paying guest?" she said with an effort at humour.

"Until you make up your mind what to do with your life."

Here was her opportunity to tell him that she already had a role in society. Yet the words would not come out and she began to tremble, sensing something that until this moment she had never remotely guessed.

"There's no need to cry," he said gently, and put his arms around her shoulders. "Live day by day and let the future take care of itself."

"You're being very trite," she mumbled against his jacket.

"A remark becomes trite because it's so good that it's been said many times before."

"What's good about my staying here?"

"You'll be with me!" he laughed, and moving her away from him, gave her a little shake. "You've always been a little spitfire, Nicky. Don't spoil it by going all tearful and docile!"

She looked at him for a long moment, her mind a whirl of frightening thoughts which, even as they settled into place, formed a picture that frightened her even more.

She was in love with Barnaby Grayson.

With a little sob she turned and ran from the room.

CHAPTER SEVEN

Whatever it was that Barney said to Joanna, it only served to increase her antagonism towards Nicola, and though she offered no more suggestions as to jobs, she went out of her way to make it clear that Nicola's presence in the hostel was robbing someone else of a badly-needed place.

Because she knew there was some justification in this, Nicola had to fight a sense of guilt at remaining here, and told herself she would return to Belgravia as soon as she had established a real relationship with Barnaby. Only when this happened would she be able to tell him who she was, and not till he knew her true identity would she leave. Yet for the moment she was no nearer to altering his attitude than she had ever been, and it remained friendly, interested, but by no stretch of the imagination any different from what it had always been.

It was Joanna who unwittingly helped to change this. Commenting bitterly that if Nicola intended to stay at the hostel indefinitely she should at least have the decency to do some extra work, she prompted Nicola to offer her services as cook.

It was an offer Nicola regretted the moment she was faced with having to plan a meal for twenty-five people. Having watched her own chef from time to time, she would have been able to make a passable dish providing she had a larder full of food, but she found it almost impossible to do anything with the unappetising hunk of meat and sack of potatoes with which she was faced. For nearly half an hour she debated what to do, refusing to think of the large, white-tiled larder in her own home with its two freezers and huge refrigerators burgeoning with prime cut sirloin steaks, fresh vegetables and fruit flown to London twice a week from Rosten farms in southern Europe. Rummaging in one of the cupboards, she found a large hand-mincer, and two back-breaking hours later had turned the meat into mince. Several large onions, which she found lurking in a wooden box on the larder floor, were also minced in with it, with the liberal addition of nutmeg and cinnamon – the only two spices she was able to discover – and which were normally used for the rice pudding which made a weekly appearance as hostel fare.

Cooking for so many people was more tedious than she had anticipated, and as she cut and sliced potatoes ready to sauté them, she looked longingly at the ironing cupboard. Even ironing sheets seemed preferable to what she was doing now.

But later that night, with dinner successfully served and a replete group of people crowded round the table, she felt an enormous sense of satisfaction at a job well done.

"Best looking meat-balls I've ever had," one of the young men said. "They tasted foreign."

"It was the seasoning," said Gillian, and looked at Nicola. "Where did you learn to cook like that?"

"In the orphanage," she mumbled, and avoiding Barnaby's gaze.

"We never got grub like that in *our* orphanage."

"I think Nicky's orphanage was rather special," Joanna intervened, her voice placid but her look malicious. "You're a very capable cook, Nicky, I'm sure you could earn your living at it."

"I've seen loads of jobs like that advertised," Carole remarked. "You know the sort of thing – elderly widower requires cook-housekeeper."

"What does she have to keep apart from the house?" asked Frank, newest resident at the hostel.

"An old man happy," said Gillian.

81

"I'm sure you could do that very well," Joanna murmured so quietly that only Nicola could hear.

With an effort Nicola kept her expression blank, though her fingers itched to feel Joanna's cheek beneath them. The feeling grew stronger as the girl left the kitchen with Barnaby, walking up the stairs beside him in a way that indicated greater closeness yet to come. There was no doubt Joanna had truly inveigled herself into every aspect of his life. Not only did she know of his work at the hospital, but she was a close part of his work here. How hard she was trying to get him to say the one word that would enable her to enter his life completely.

"Don't you like our dishes?" Gillian asked Nicola. "From the way you're banging them together I get the feeling you'd like to smash them!"

"I'd like to smash *something*."

"Joanna's head, I suppose." And then, at Nicola's startled look: "We all fall for Barnaby sooner or later. But don't worry — it doesn't last."

"You sound very sure," commented Nicola.

"I am. This place is a shelter, and he's the head of it. It's natural we should turn to him; women always love anyone who protects them. It's part of their heritage — goes back to the days when men did the hunting and killing and women stayed in the caves."

"Where did you learn that?"

"Barnaby was talking about it this afternoon when Elaine said she fell in love with him the first week she arrived."

"You mean he knows that the — that the girls here usually fall for him?"

"Sure. There isn't much that escapes his notice."

Nicola found the thought mortifying; not only because it meant Barnaby must know how she felt, but because he had made no response to it. But then he was too ethical to do so.

Despite his assertion that she should not regard herself as a patient of his, the very fact that she was here, under his aegis, would preclude him from allowing himself to have any emotional feeling towards her. Only when she was no longer here would he be free to see her in the way he wanted. Yet how *did* he want to see her? She was no nearer knowing this today than she had been last week. She had to make him aware of her as a woman. Once she had done this, she would not be afraid to tell him her real name.

"I'm surprised Barnaby remained single all these years." She did not realise she had spoken her thoughts aloud until she hard Gillian laugh.

"Joanna's trying to remedy that. She's around him all the time." Gillian retrieved a plate before Nicola could bang it on the table. "Go up and watch the telly," she advised. "You look flaked out after all your cooking."

Nicola escaped upstairs. Laughter came from the common-room, and unwilling to make any more conversation she stood in the hall wondering what to do.

The door of the small sitting room opened and Barnaby stood looking at her. "What's the problem, Nicky?"

"Not tired enough for bed but too tired to join in all that." She jerked her head behind her.

"Come and sit with me," he said. "I'm listening to some music."

"I can't see Nicky enjoying Bach." Joanna had come to stand beside him, tall and slim and very sure of herself.

Nicola drew herself up to her full five feet. "I was hoping Barnaby would play me the *Teddy Bears' Picnic*," she retorted.

Barnaby's mouth twitched, but his face remained serious as he moved Joanna back into the room and waited for Nicola to join them.

Ensconced on the lumpy settee, she found it worse having to watch Joanna smile enticingly at Barnaby than it would have been to stay in the other sitting room without him, and only the knowledge that her presence here was a considerable irritation to Joanna enabled her to remain.

A Bach fugue came to an end and Barnaby removed it from the record player. "That was Joanna's choice," he said pleasantly. "What's yours, Nicky?"

"What have you got?"

"Come and see."

Reluctantly she went to stand beside him, tumultuously aware of the warmth emanating from him. It was an essentially masculine warmth, compounded of after-shave lotion, hair cream – not that he appeared to use any – and pipe tobacco. Hurriedly she looked through the records, surprised at how many there were. "You've got a big selection."

"I've been collecting for years."

"Is this house your home?"

"It *is* now. I used to have a flat the other side of Chelsea, but I spend so much time here it was a waste of money keeping it on."

Aware of Joanna watching them, she bent over the records again and then handed him one.

He looked at it and smiled. "Feeling in that sort of mood?"

She nodded and sat down without answering. But as the strains of Tchaikovsky's *Romeo and Juliet Overture* filled the air, she regretted her choice, for the haunting sadness of the violins brought tears to her eyes.

Only as the music came to an end did Joanna shatter the mood by saying she had stopped being a Tchaikovsky fan from the age of fourteen. "He's so sentimental," she asserted.

"There's nothing wrong with sentiment," Barnaby replied, lounging back in his chair. "It's your choice now, Joanna."

84

"I think I'll go home."

At once he stood up and made for the door. "There's no need for you to go, Nicky," he said over his shoulder. "Stay here and play some more music."

The door closed behind him and Joanna, and Nicola jumped up, too angry and humiliated to sit still. It was hopeless to try and make Barnaby notice her while she was living here, and again she toyed with the idea of leaving. She moved across to the chair he had just vacated and stretched out in it. A standard lamp was the only illumination and the bulk of the room was in shadow, apart from the gentle flicker of flames in the grate. She flexed fingers still aching from peeling potatoes, and made herself more comfortable, too tired to get up and put on another record, too tired even to find the energy to go to bed. With a sigh she closed her eyes.

An instinctive awareness of being watched brought her back to consciousness. Slowly she lifted her lids and beneath the tangle of lashes saw Barnaby watching her. She struggled into a sitting position, aware that the ribbon confining her hair had worked loose, and that the dark strands lay like a silky cloud around her shoulders. Half-heartedly she pushed it off her face and sat up even straighter. "I fell asleep," she said unnecessarily.

"You're tired from cooking."

"It *was* rather much," she admitted.

"Because you were determined to show off."

"I wanted to make something nice," she said, stung to tears by his remark.

"Even though it meant exhausting yourself? A stew would have gone down just as well and not left you looking as pale as an unlit candle."

"I'm sorry my looks don't please you," she muttered.

"Come now," he chided, "you know your looks please me

very much. I just don't like to see you working unnecessarily hard."

"I did it for you," she said without thinking.

"I know."

She was glad the room was in shadow. "What else do you know?"

"That you're a tired little girl who should be in bed."

"I'm not a —"

"Little girl," he finished for her, and leaning forward drew her to her feet. From his expression, tender and teasing, she knew the gesture was prompted by kindness, but as his hands touched hers her own emotion communicated itself to him, and his grip tightened. "Don't look at me like that," he said huskily.

"Like what?"

"Like Circe. It's those big grey-green eyes of yours. They're more green than grey tonight — that's because there's more of the witch in you."

"It's the witching hour," she said.

"Time for good little girls to be in bed."

"And bad little girls?"

"They're in bed too."

"Not on their own."

The smile left his face and momentarily it looked blank. "But you're a good little girl *now*," he said.

"I always have been."

He did not answer and, aware of his doubt, she grew angry. "Don't you know the sort of person I am?" she cried. "I thought you prided yourself on being a good judge of character."

"I'm sorry."

His apology was not what she had expected, and as though realising it, he forced himself to continue. "We weren't going

86

to talk about your past any more, remember? We're only going to think of your future."

"What future do you see for me?"

"A happy one."

"With whom?" she whispered.

"A young man who'll come into your life one day."

Angry that he did not know that the man was already standing beside her, she turned sharply away from him. Her foot caught in a threadbare patch of the carpet and she stumbled. His hand came out to save her and she fell against him, her slight weight resting in the curve of his arm. She turned to free herself, but he moved too, and unwittingly she found herself facing him again, but much closer to him this time. Without being able to stop herself she put her arms around his neck. For an instant he resisted, then with a stifled sound he pulled her close and buried his head in her hair. His lips were warm on her scalp and her heart began to thump heavily, so that she trembled and clung to him the more.

"Kiss me," she cried, and raised her face to his.

Silently he did so. For so big and assured a man, his kiss astonished her by its gentleness, and she wound her arm about his neck and pulled his head lower. She felt him tremble and only then realised that his gentleness was caused by his control. "Kiss me properly," she whispered, and pressed closer.

In her long search for someone to love she had found herself wrong many times, but so sure was she of Barnaby's character that she felt no embarrassment with him. Here at last was someone she could love without wondering if he was holding her in his arms because she was Nicola Rosten, heiress, and this knowledge filled her with such exultation that it swept away her reserve and she nestled against him like a homing pigeon.

"For God's sake, Nicky, don't!" The thudding of his heart

belied his actions as he tried to push her away.

"Why not? You want to kiss me. You know you do!"

"I mustn't."

"Why not? I'm not a patient of yours."

"But you're staying here . . . it's wrong. Nicky, please!"

"I'm the one to say please," she murmured, and raising herself on tiptoe, pulled his head down again.

"You can't say you're not asking for it," he said huskily, and this time made no effort to hold his desire in check.

His kiss was one of unleashed passion, his lips forcing hers apart. Her trembling body aroused him to an even greater desire and the kiss deepened, drawing a response from her she had not known she possessed.

His hands twined themselves through her hair and then moved on to encircle her waist, coming up beneath her sweater to caress her curving breasts. They swelled beneath his touch and she clung to him more tightly, longing to surrender completely but knowing she could not do so while there were still secrets between them.

"Barnaby," she breathed. "Darling . . ."

He jerked at the sound of her voice, and with the movements of an automaton pulled her hands away from his neck and forced them down to her sides.

"No, Nicky, this is madness." His voice was low. "We'll regret it in the morning."

"I won't!" she cried passionately.

"You will," he asserted, and stepped away from her. "Nicky, stop it!"

Tears blinded her eyes. "Don't you *want* me?"

"That question shows a basic ignorance of biology!"

"Stop teasing," she cried. "Can't you be serious about anything?"

"Not this," he replied. "It's too dangerous."

"Don't you ever let yourself go?"

"At the right time and the right place."

"And with the right girl, I suppose. You've made it pretty obvious it wouldn't be me."

"Now you're talking like the child you're always telling me you're not. You know very well why I stopped kissing you – and you wouldn't have respected me very much if I hadn't stopped."

"I don't want respect," she whispered. "I want *you.* You know how I feel about you."

"I know what you think you feel." He put out a hand as though to touch her cheek, then gave a half smile and moved over to the far side of the fireplace. "Don't confuse being grateful with being in love. At the moment you see me as your saviour and you're reacting accordingly. But when you've made another life for yourself – with people of your own age – you'll feel quite different."

"You talk as if you're Methuselah!"

"I'm thirty-four. Young when compared with your Marty, of course, but –"

"No!" she cried, and stopped. It was ridiculous to let Barnaby go on believing she had been in love with a man old enough to be her grandfather – and a butler, to boot. Unable to stop herself, she smiled, though she was unaware of it until she saw the puzzlement on Barnaby's face.

"What's the joke, Nicky?"

"That you should believe I was in love with Marty. None of it's true," she blurted out. "He isn't –"

"I know you didn't love him," Barnaby interrupted. "You wanted a good time and he was able to give it to you. You don't need to apologise for it."

Helplessly she stared at him. Did he really see her as a girl who would sell herself for a good time? Anger against him welled up in her, made more bitter by knowing how desperately she wanted him to believe in her despite all evidence to the contrary. "I'm a fool," she thought ironically. As Nicola Rosten she had wanted to be loved regardless of her wealth, and as Nicky Rose she wanted to be loved regardless of the life she was supposed to have led. Somehow she seemed to find it impossible to put herself in a situation where she could be judged for what she was.

"You told me to forget my past and think only of my future," she reminded him. "Why can't you do the same?"

"I'm trying."

"I'm surprised you find it so hard."

"I'm surprised too," he said enigmatically, and went to the door. "Good night, Nicky. Sleep well."

She followed him out and slowly climbed the stairs, puzzled by his last remark and wishing with all her heart that she could read his mind.

CHAPTER EIGHT

For several days Barnaby went out of his way to avoid being alone with Nicola. At first she saw his behaviour as regret for having kissed her, but gradually she sensed a different motivation behind it; sensed it not so much through his avoidance of her but through his obvious tension when they were in the same room.

In his position of father-figure to a constant stream of neurotic girls, several of them must have thrown themselves at his head in order to gain his attention. This being so, it was surprising that he should display symptoms of acute embarrassment whenever she was near him. Had he not been emotionally aroused by her, he would not surely have done so. She gained comfort from this; as she also did from the knowledge that from their very first meeting he had shown an interest in her far beyond his normal one. Joanna's antagonism towards her was additional proof of this.

Convinced that Barnaby's aloofness was a covering to protect himself, she was happier than she had been in her life, and spurred on by this, tackled all her chores with unusual willingness. The much-disliked ironing was dispensed with speed, if not efficiency, and she would stand blithely at the sink wallowing in sudsy water and a welter of dishes.

It was here, in a steamy kitchen, with foam up to her elbows, that Barnaby finally faced her alone. He had spent the day at hospital, and as always when he did so, he liked to have an hour to himself to marshal his thoughts. Usually he remained in his sitting room or bedroom for an hour, and she could not hide her surprise at seeing him in front of her now.

"I didn't expect to find you washing up so late." His voice was normal and easy.

"One of the boys had an epileptic fit and it upset the lunch hour. Joanna's taken him to the hospital."

"So that's why she isn't here."

Nicola nodded. "She rang through to say she wouldn't be back till later this evening."

"I'll call and tell her not to come back at all." He frowned. "It's ridiculous for her to spend so much time here. She has no life of her own."

"The *hostel's* her life – the way it's yours." Nicola took her hands out of the suds. "Would you like some tea?"

"I can make it myself." His smile robbed the words of terseness. "I'll make you a cup too. You look as though you need one."

Aware of the sudden light in his eyes, her heart started to race and she hurriedly dried the plates while he made the tea.

"For heaven's sake leave the dishes and come and sit down," he said with an irritability she had never before heard from him.

"Someone has to do them," she pointed out.

"What about the other girls? Whenever I see you, you're working." He pushed a cup towards her. "Why do you let them use you?" he said furiously. "You're so little, I suppose they think they can take advantage of you."

"Of course not. The trouble is, I'm so slow, everything I do takes me twice as long as it should."

"I'd have thought you'd be used to washing-up and house-work."

"I never did any before I came here."

"Are you telling me that ladies' maids are treated like ladies too?" he asked humorously.

"*I* was."

"Must have been as good as being Miss Rosten herself."

"It was."

He put two lumps of sugar in his tea and stirred it thoughtfully. "Not hankering to go back there, are you?"

"I'd give anything to be back in my own bed," she said truthfully, then added: "It was extremely comfortable, living there. No expense spared, and all that sort of thing."

"Spare me the details," he said drily. "I couldn't care less how the other half lives. I've enough trouble coping with my own half."

"You cope very well. Too well. That's why you do too much."

"Don't start telling me again how tired I look! Remember what happened the last time you did."

Warmth suffused her body. "I was wondering if *you'd* forgotten. You've tried to give me that impression."

"From self-defence. You've a habit of getting under a man's skin."

"You make me sound like a disease."

"You could easily become one with me."

"I'd like that."

"Stop it," he said in rough but kindly tones. "You've got to go out and make a life for yourself. You can't spend it here washing and ironing."

"I certainly can't," she said fervently.

"What I mean is, you're intelligent enough to do something worthwhile; take a training course, learn shorthand and typing perhaps."

"That costs money."

"We've a few Trusts who give us funds. I'm pretty certain I

can get some help for you."

She looked at her teacup, intensely aware of him sprawled in the chair opposite, his thick hair falling across his forehead in the way she knew so well, his eyebrows lowered over those piercing grey eyes. "You talk as if you'd like to get rid of me, Barnaby."

"It isn't good for you to remain here."

"Do you *want* me to go?"

"I want what's best for you."

She looked him full in the face. "What would you say if I told you *you* were best for me?"

"I'd say you were too young to know your own mind."

"I'm twenty-one," she retorted, "and I bet I've seen more of the world than *you*!"

"Travelling as Miss Rosten's maid, I suppose? That's not seeing the world, Nicky. Nor will it help you develop as a person."

"What about sitting at a desk typing? The only thing *that* will develop is my rear end!"

He smiled. "There's other work. Or you can study at night school or a polytechnic."

Irritated by his determination to get rid of her, she lashed out at him, "If those are your best suggestions I'd rather go back to Marty!"

With an exclamation Barnaby stood up. His anger was unmistakable and she thrilled to it, knowing she had hit him where he was most vulnerable. Poor darling, she thought tenderly, if only he would stop fighting his attraction to her. With silent steps she reached his side and placed herself between him and the door.

"Don't you like me a little bit, Barnaby?"

"More than a little bit," he said roughly.

"Then why are you afraid to say so?"

"We've already discussed why. Things haven't changed since then."

"You're very hard."

Her lips trembled and he reached out and caught her shoulder. "Don't cry, Nicky. You're such a little thing, I can see why men want to protect you. But you must learn to depend on yourself – not use your beauty to . . ."

He withdrew his hand and put it into the pocket of his jacket, moving slightly back as though afraid to come too close to her. But she pressed forward, refusing to let him get away.

"Did you mean what you just said – that you think I'm beautiful?"

Hearing herself pose the question she wanted to laugh; that she, Nicola Rosten, who had never lacked admirers ready to heap praise on her, should be asking such a thing of a tired, overworked doctor who was doing everything he could to send her away from him.

"I never answer leading questions," he replied.

"One day I'll make you."

There were footsteps behind them and Frank came in. "Carole's asking for you," he said to Barnaby.

"I'll go up and see her."

He hurried out and Frank poured himself a cup of tea.

"You seemed pretty involved with Barnaby. Fancy him, do you?"

"Yes – just like all the other girls here!" She put the dirty cups in the sink, noticing how rough her hands were. Next time she went to a fancy dress party she'd go as Madame Pompadour. It was certain to lead to more interesting experiences than the ones she was having here.

"What you grinning at?" Frank asked.

"Just deciding I hate being Cinderella."

"Who's the Ugly Sister – Joanna?" Without waiting for a

reply, he went on: "Now there's a girl I'd fancy. I'm sure there's fire beneath that icy surface."

"I doubt it. She's ice to the core."

"Not with Barnaby. You should have seen her this morning when she was planning his present."

"What present?"

"For his birthday. It's next week."

"What's she buying him?" Nicola asked with heavy casualness.

"A gallon of paint and ten yards of orange material." Seeing Nicola's disbelief, he explained that several of them were going to refurbish Barnaby's sitting room. "Joanna's supplying the cash and *we're* doing the strong arm stuff. Gillian's making the curtains and Carole's doing the covering for his settee and armchair. The rest of us are painting."

Nicola was furious that Joanna had hit upon such a good idea, and fleetingly thought of all *she* could do for him. Buy him a crocodile wallet to replace his shabby leather one, and a wafer-thin gold watch instead of the chunky one that covered his broad wrist. Savile Row suits, of course, and an Aston Martin. Even as the ideas welled inside her she knew he would accept nothing from her. What was it he had said during one of their group discussions? "There has to be equality between two people before a relationship can develop. If one person gives and the other one takes, the balance is destroyed."

His remark had provoked considerable argument – his remarks generally did – and though he frequently made an assertion in order to cause a discussion, she was sure he had meant *that* particular statement.

"No good asking *you* to help with the painting," Frank interrupted her thoughts. "You're no bigger than a brush yourself!"

She rounded on him with a soapy hand and he swung her up

into his arms and twirled her round until she squealed to be let down.

Breathlessly she smoothed her hair away from her face, wondering what Marty would say if he saw her now. With a pang of fear she remembered she had promised to call him again if she didn't, he was more than likely to come down and see what was happening to her.

How horrified he would be at his first sight of the hostel. It was a far cry from the warmth and opulence of Belgravia, yet she had been happier here than in her own home. Not only because of Barnaby, but because of the camaraderie she had developed with the young men and women staying here. Their unhappy past lives and uncertain future had made her realise how lucky her own life was, and she vowed that when she returned to it she would do something useful with the money that was increasingly amassing to her. No longer would it suffice to sign cheques giving away thousands of pounds to charities designated by Marty or her legal advisers. From now on she wanted to know what those charities did and how they were controlled. She might even set up her own trust.

The thought grew in her mind like a well-fertilized seed, and burst into bloom even as it settled. How much Barnaby would be able to achieve with her money! He would no longer need to worry about the upkeep of one hostel when he could afford to have ten, twenty, a hundred even. There was no end to what they could achieve together!

Elated at what the future held, she slipped on a cardigan and hurried out to telephone Marty. It was too dangerous to call from the office in case Barnaby overheard her again.

Feeling like a prisoner who had just been released, she sped along the street. Most of the houses were large and shabby, but a few had been re-developed into elegant homes for the professional classes. What a curious mixture this part of London was, with rich people living hugger-mugger with poor. The only common denominator was the silver-grey ribbon of the Thames that wound its way majestically along one side of the Borough.

Its nearness to the river was the nicest part of the hostel, for when she lay in her room at night she could enjoy the mournful hoot of a barge or the chug of a river police boat, its beam flashing across the black water.

But this afternoon the river was asleep and the boats rocked gently at their moorings. The seats along the Embankment were deserted too, with only an occasional occupant huddled in a corner, coat collar turned up against the wind. It was a different story at night; then the benches were occupied by vagrants trying to catch a few hours' sleep before the policeman on the beat would waken them and set them on their way again. It was incredible to think that thousands of men and women slept rough each night, many of them doing so from choice rather than necessity.

But these were not the people Barnaby wished to help. His concern was with the young who, because of their inability to cope with their emotional problems, had run away from them and now needed help in order to stop running.

The thought made her stop running too, and she looked round for a telephone kiosk. A group of three stood like red guards ahead of her and she made for them.

Moments later she put down the receiver in disappointment. Marty was out and the butler did not know when he would be back. She had left her name with the butler, but she knew Marty would not be satisfied until he had spoken to her himself, and somewhat dejectedly she began to retrace her steps.

On her right she glimpsed the Kings Road and impulsively she walked towards it. It seemed an age since she had looked into a shop window and she enjoyed staring at pretty dresses and suits which, a few weeks ago, would not even have merited a glance from her. A bookshop caught her eye and she paused to look at the beautifully bound volumes. Several of them were open to show magnificent colour plates, and on an impulse she went in.

Only as she saw the frigid expression on the face of the young man by the counter did she realise that he thought she had come inside to get out of the cold. With her pale, well-scrubbed face and tiny figure hidden beneath a shapeless mass of wool, she gave no indication of being a potential buyer.

"Can I help you?" he enquired, conveying the impression that he knew it was a waste of his time to do so.

"I'd like to see some art books." Her modulated voice merited a keen glance from him, but her shabbiness won, and with obvious disinclination he moved to one of the shelves.

"Which artist are you interested in? We have an extensive stock."

Nicola thought of the colourful paintings in Barnaby's bedroom and wished she knew more of his taste. One thing was certain – he liked colour and strong line.

"Do you have a book on Gauguin?"

"A folio of his best work has just been printed. A limited edition, I'm afraid, and very expensive."

"I'd like to see it."

Reluctantly he retired to the back of the shop and returned with a large, hand-tooled leather book. Some two dozen reproductions of Gauguin's most colourful paintings were magnificently reproduced, and she stared at his portrayal of Christ, the brilliant simplicity of the figure on the cross outlined so poignantly by a limpid sky.

"Beautiful," she murmured. "How much is it?"

"A hundred and fifty pounds."

"I haven't any money with me, but I definitely want to buy
99

it. Can you keep it for me?"

"Not without a deposit."

She racked her brains for a solution. Her only hope was to call Marty again. Giving the young man her warmest smile – which made him revise his earlier opinion that she was a plain little thing – she begged him to hold the folio till tomorrow, when she promised to send someone along with the money.

"Very well, madame, I'll keep it till noon. But not any later."

Flashing him another smile, she went out. It was already late afternoon and street lamps cast yellow pools of light on pavements damp with rain. The headlamps of cars sparkled in the drizzle and she hurried across the road. A loud hooter made her jump, and glancing at the saloon car from where it came, she saw a man gesticulating furiously.

"Nicola," he called. "Don't you know me?"

"Marty!" With a cry she wrenched open the door and slipped into the front seat beside him. "I never expected to see you here."

"I was on my way to the hostel."

"You weren't!"

"I certainly was."

The lights changed and he turned off the main street and parked in a side turning. Skewing round in his seat he looked at her, a man of sixty with the upright bearing of a soldier and the keen glance of an astute business man, both of which he had been in his time.

"Do you know it's more than two weeks since you called me?"

"Actually it's only an hour. I telephoned just before, but you were out."

"On my way to see you," he said testily. "I've been worried out of my wits." He peered at her. "You're very pale."

100

"No make-up."

"What's happened to your eyes?"

"No mascara!"

He barked a laugh. "I never thought I'd live to see the day."

"Nor did I," she confessed, and smiled at him.

He softened visibly. "Actually you look remarkably well. Though your – er – clothes don't do much for you."

"You've never noticed my clothes before," she said.

"Dior doesn't need commenting on!" he said ironically, and patted her cheek. "Now that we're finally face to face, perhaps you'll tell me how long you intend going on with this masquerade?"

"As long as it takes me to make Barnaby realise he loves me as much as I love him."

The silence that met this remark could have been cut with a knife. "I would be obliged if you would explain yourself," said Mr. George Martin in his most Mr. Martin voice.

"Don't be stuffy, Marty. You know exactly what I mean." Seeing the explosion about to erupt, she said quickly: "I'm in love with Barnaby Grayson."

"And who is *he*? Some vagrant you've picked up?"

"He's the doctor who started the hostel," she explained, and went on to tell him all she knew of Barnaby. When one was with him his background did not matter, yet she knew her godfather – not knowing him – would need something concrete on which to base his judgment. Carefully she recounted all she had ever gleaned about Barnaby Grayson's life; only son of a heart specialist who had died when Barnaby had been at medical school, and a politically conscious mother who devoted herself to social work and from whom he had obviously absorbed a great deal of his thinking.

"Good yeoman stock," she concluded jauntily. "No coronets in the cupboard, but no skeletons either!"

"He's an improvement on Jeffrey," George Martin said. "But not the man for you."

"How can you say that when you don't know him?"

"I know *you.*"

Tears filled her eyes and she dashed them away, surprised she should be so emotional that a few discouraging words from Marty could make her cry.

"It seems I didn't come in search of you any too soon," he said crisply. "Be sensible, my dear. I'm sure Doctor Grayson is an admirable man, but his life is quite different from yours."

"That's why I love him. He's made something of his life and he's helping other people to make something of theirs. What have *I* ever done for anyone?"

"You give jobs to – thousands of people."

"Rosten Foods," she said bitterly. "That'll go on whether I'm dead or alive!"

"It will go on much longer if you produce an heir," George Martin said drily. "How do you think Doctor Grayson would fit into the Rosten background?"

"I'm more concerned with how I'd fit into his! Don't you understand what I'm trying to tell you, Marty? I've changed. I'm not the girl I was. I can't go back to my old life. It's empty and dull."

"You used to keep telling me it was wonderful."

"I was pretending."

"And now you're not? How can you be sure, Nicola?"

She sought for the right words, but failed to find them. "I *am* sure," she said at last. "I can't explain, but I *am* sure."

Several seconds passed while George Martin looked at her.

"It's the first time I've known you at a loss for words," he said finally. "Perhaps you've found your Mecca after all."

He went to switch on the engine, but she put out her hand. "You can't drive me back to the hostel. They'd wonder who you were."

"You don't intend keeping on with this masquerade?"

"I've got to find the right time to tell Barnaby. He isn't going to like it when he finds out who I am. He thinks rich people are worthless."

"Don't tell me he'll be annoyed because you're Nicola Rosten?"

"He'll be furious to begin with," she replied. "But mainly because I tricked him. Once he sees the funny side of it, he won't mind about my money. Just think what I can do to help him!"

"I'd leave *him* to think of that," Marty said drily.

"He isn't a fortune-hunter."

"He can't be, if he's fallen in love with you the way you are." Marty peered at her. "I assume he *does* reciprocate your feelings?"

"He hasn't — he hasn't admitted it yet. But that's because he thinks he's too old for me."

"I'm sure you'll be able to make him change his mind!"

"I'm sure too," she said confidently.

"How much longer do you intend staying here?"

"It's Barnaby's birthday next week. I'll tell him then." She gave a little gasp. "That reminds me, could you let me have some money?"

She explained why she wanted it and Marty shook his head. "I doubt if they'll accept a cheque from you — not with you looking like a homeless stray. I'd better give it to the shop myself."

Gratefully she directed him there, and tried to hide her amusement at the young man's discomfiture when he received George Martin's cheque.

About to take the book with her, she changed her mind. It was too large to hide in her room and there was no other place to keep it. Besides, she did not want anyone asking where she had obtained the money to buy such an expensive gift. When she gave it to Barnaby she would tell him who she was, but for the moment she dared not risk taking it to the hostel.

"Please keep it for a couple of days," she asked the assistant. "I'll call back for it."

Outside the shop again it was raining heavily, and Marty caught her arm.

"I'm not letting you walk back in weather like this. At least let me drive you to the bottom of the road."

Reluctantly she agreed, her fear increasing as they neared the hostel, and her godfather had barely turned the car into the road before she made him stop.

"When will I be seeing you?" he asked, drawing the car into the curb.

"Some time next week."

He frowned. "There are some papers I need you to sign."

"Can't they wait?"

"No. It's a contract from America and it must be returned at once. It's being flown over on Sunday."

"Can you meet me with it on Monday when I collect the book? Then I won't have to leave the hostel twice."

"You talk as if you're a prisoner."

"It's a prison of my own making!" She held out her hands. "Look – from dishwashing!"

It was a long while since she had her godfather so surprised. "You're more than in love with this Grayson," he said gruffly. "You must be besotted with the fellow!"

"I am." She hugged him and then scrambled from the car. "Goodbye, Marty, I'll be seeing you soon."

As usual the door of the hostel was unlatched and she entered the hall and stood for a moment looking at its beige walls. Voices came from the sitting room and she knew Barnaby was coming near to the end of one of his discussions. Not wishing to see him until she had made herself tidy, she ran to her room and combed her hair, deciding not to put it back into its usual ponytail. She had already got Barnaby to admit he found her beautiful and if she could get him alone again this evening she might be able to encourage him further, might even make him admit he loved her. Humming softly under her breath, she went downstairs.

The sitting room was already emptying, and several people were going down to the kitchen, but Nicola remained where she was, waiting for Barnaby.

He came into the hall, but before she could reach him the front door opened and Joanna came in. The wind had whipped her cheeks, but the gleam in her eyes came from spite.

"So you've come back to the hostel, Nicky. Or have you only returned to collect your things?"

"Why should I collect my things?" Nicola asked.

"Aren't you going back to your boy-friend – or should I say your elderly friend? He can hardly be called a boy!"

"What are you trying to say, Joanna?" Barnaby interrupted sharply.

"Just that you're wasting your time with Nicky. She's playing you for a fool. She's just come from a rendezvous with Marty!"

Barnaby looked directly at Nicola. "Is this true?"

"I – I –" she began.

"Of course it's true," Joanna interrupted. "I saw her getting out of his car and I heard what she said to him." The bright

105

brown eyes brimmed with malicious pleasure. " 'Goodbye, Marty, I'll be seeing you soon!' " Joanna swung back to Barnaby. "There's no need for you to ask if I'm telling the truth. Just look at your little Nicky's face and see for yourself!"

CHAPTER NINE

It seemed an eternity, though it was barely a few seconds while Barnaby came slowly to the centre of the hall to look directly into Nicola's face.

"Is it true?" he repeated. "Are you going back to Marty?"

"No. I met him by accident. I went out for a walk and – and – he found me."

"It was hardly an accident on *his* part."

"Maybe not," she said slowly. "He was probably driving round here hoping to – hoping to catch a glimpse of me."

"I suppose he wants you back?"

"He'd like me to leave the hostel," she admitted, "but not to – not to go back to him. He knows *that*'s over."

"Pull the other leg, Nicky," Joanna said rudely. "I saw the way you threw your arms around him before you left the car."

Nicola lowered her eyes, wishing she could have the pleasure of wringing Joanna's slim white neck. What bad luck that it had been her – of all people – who had seen her leave Marty's car. She had been so careful to make sure the way was clear before she had opened the door to get out, but then Marty had stopped her to discuss the contract, and when she had finally left him she forgotten to re-check that no one was around.

"It's obvious she planned the meeting," Joanna spoke directly to Barnaby. "It's ridiculous to let her go on staying here. She's just taking the place of someone who's in real need of help."

"How do you know *I* don't need help?" Nicky blurted out, her fury with Joanna letting her imagination run away with her. "It isn't easy to cut somebody out of your life and never see them again. You're not dealing with characters in a book – you're dealing with people!"

Barnaby glanced at her, his expression cold, before he turned to Joanna. "Nicky's right. Things aren't always as cut and dried as you'd like them to be."

"She's making a fool of you," Joanna retorted. "A fool!"

"I'm not!" Nicola put her hand on Barnaby's arm. "Believe me, Barnaby, I'm not!"

"There's no need to get upset." His voice was gentle, but he stepped back a pace, the movement serving to loosen Nicola's grasp. "You'd better go down to dinner, or there won't be any left."

Her lips trembled, but she forced herself to keep calm. "What about you?"

"Joanna will bring me something on a tray."

He went back into the sitting room and Joanna turned a triumphant gaze on Nicola. Afraid that if she remained within striking distance she might do exactly that, Nicola made for the comfort of the overcrowded kitchen.

It was impossible even to pretend she had an appetite, and she nibbled at some bread and made herself a cup of tea. The desire to tell Barnaby the truth was a strong one, and she was only prevented from doing so by the fear that – having not yet admitted he loved her – he might never do so once he discovered her real identity. The confidence with which she had told Marty he loved her had been more an assertion of what she wished to believe, than what she knew to be the truth and, faced with the possibility of having to prove what she had said, she knew she dared not do so yet.

If only Barnaby would stop fighting her and admit he wanted her! Yet he was still bound by the conventions of medical etiquette, despite his assertion that she was not a patient of his nor under his vigilance. Perhaps this would always be the case while she was in the hostel. But she dared not leave it for fear he would not come after her. No, she had to make him realise he loved her.

She closed her eyes, the better to bring him into focus. How totally different he was from all the other men she had known! There were times when she could cheerfully murder him for all the irritating things he did: his unfailing humour regardless of the situation; his calm that nothing seemed to ruffle; his logical mind that cut away all false emotions to get to the root of the problem, and the stupid way in which he was working himself to death by long hours in the hospital and a leisure spent at the beck and call of everyone here. The urge to seek him out was so strong that she half-rose in her chair, but settled back again as she remembered Joanna was with him.

Joanna of the soft voice and hard eyes. The kindly helpmate who wanted to be his soulmate.

Nerves at fever pitch, she kept her ears tuned to any sounds coming from upstairs, and was grateful when several of the young men and girls decided to return to the living room. If she went with them she would be able to hear when Joanna left.

Slowly the evening passed, the hours punctuated by conversation and records, and it was past ten when she heard the front door slam. Peering casually through the front window she saw Joanna climb into her small white Renault and drive off. Without giving herself time to think, she sped across the hall, knocked on his door and went in. The look on his face told her he had been expecting her.

"Explanations aren't necessary," he said gently before she could speak.

"*You* mightn't want them," she retorted, "but *I* want to give them!"

He waited rocking backwards and forwards on the balls of his feet. He had changed from a suit into slacks and sweater, a dark blue one which she had never seen before. It made his skin look paler and gave a more reddish tinge to his hair.

"You must be the most untidy doctor in the hospital," she burst out.

"Was that the explanation?"

"You know very well it isn't!"

"Then I suggest we leave my appearance alone and concentrate on yours. I assume you came in to tell me that appearances are not always what they seem?"

"They're not what Joanna made them seem. I didn't arrange to meet Marty. It was an accident."

"On your part, maybe. But he obviously had every intention of seeing *you*. He wants you to leave the hostel, I suppose?"

"Yes."

"What did you say?"

Nicola looked him fully in the face. They were only a few feet apart and she could see the reflection of the firelight in his eyes. "I told him I was happy here and would never go back to my old way of living." Since this was exactly what she had told Marty she was able to speak with sincerity, and it shone from her eyes which, limpid as forest pools, glowed up at him.

Visibly stiffening, Barnaby said: "I'm sure he tried to make you change your mind."

"He never will. From now on my life will be different."

"Do you mean that, or are you still playing the part you

think I want you to play?"

Wondering if there was a trick in the question, she considered it. "I want to be the sort of person you'd like me to be," she replied carefully. "Is that what you mean by my playing a part?"

"Not quite. You're like a chameleon, Nicky, or perhaps it would be kinder to say like a little girl wanting to be loved by her great big daddy."

"I don't see you as my father."

"Let's agree to differ about that."

"Why? It's the whole crux of the situation. I'm not a little innocent, and –"

"I never thought you were," he interposed, and her cheeks flamed as she understood his meaning.

"Why are you so quick to judge my relationship with Marty?" she flared. "I love him, but there's never been anything between us."

"If you say so," he said without expression, so that she did not know whether he believed her. "Let's not talk about it any more, Nicky; you're free to leave here any time you want, but you're equally free to stay."

"Even though I'm taking the place of some girl who might be in need of help?"

For the first time he looked angry. "Don't take any notice of Joanna. She had no right to say what she did. *I* decide who stays here, no one else."

"Will you decide when I must leave?"

"No," he said shortly. "That will be your decision."

"Then you'll never be rid of me."

"Never can be a long time."

"Time is much longer when I'm not with you."

He looked surprised. "That sounds like the lyric of a song! Maybe you should do something in journalism."

"*My Life in the Rosten House,*" she said mischievously. "That would make a good story for the Sunday papers."

"Not that sort of writing," he said so sharply that she realised he was not sure if she was joking. "I dislike people who make their living out of gossip. It's the worst form of prostitution."

She nodded vigorously, remembering how many of her formative years had been spoiled by photographers and ferret-nosed reporters. "People with a lot of money are always considered fair game for the gutter press."

"I suppose you're thinking of Miss Rosten?"

"Indeed I am. She had to be careful what she *thought* – let alone what she said."

"My heart bleeds for her!" he said unfeelingly, and walked over to the record player.

Elgar's Violin Concerto echoed sweetly in the room and Nicola listened to it entranced. The music seemed to personify her love for the rough-haired gentle man who sat opposite her. What would her friends think of him, she wondered, and what would *he* think of them? Somehow she knew he would not even bother to consider them, as she had not considered them ever since she had come here to live. It was surprising that she had given none of them any thought, not even Jeffrey, except for a few fleeting moments when she had realised how weak and facile he was compared with Barnaby. Barnaby. Even his name suited him. Strong yet tender. She gave a contented sigh and curled up comfortably on the settee. A spring dug into her and she jumped up with an ejaculation. She hoped to goodness someone would do something about the spring before putting on the new cover.

"Sit here," Barnaby said with a soft laugh, and got up from his own chair.

She shook her head, but he reached out to catch her hand

and push her into it. The touch of his fingers made her tremble, and unable to prevent herself she put her arms around him.

"Nicky, don't!"

She refused to heed him and, standing on tiptoe, kissed his chin and then pulled his head down so that she could reach his lips.

"Don't tell me to stop," she pleaded. "You know how I feel about you."

"I know how you *think* you feel."

"I *know* what I feel!" she cried. "Stop treating me like a child! I'm a woman."

"You *are*," he groaned, and suddenly stopped fighting her any more, returning her kiss with a ferocity that took her by surprise.

He made no attempt to hide his need, and the vibrant tautness of his body showed his longing for her. Her mouth moved beneath the pressure of his and his lips gently caressed hers, alive with desire as their kiss lengthened and deepened, Her whole body burned with passion, and she pressed against him until she felt the hardness of his thigh and the throbbing of his own desire.

His woman, she thought exultantly; and pressed closer still. Again and again they kissed, and though he might have called her a girl he showed in every way possible that he considered her a woman.

If only she need never leave him. A night in his arms and he would no longer be able to pretend he did not love her. Why didn't he put it into words? Almost as though he could sense her thoughts, he pushed her away from him, keeping his hands on her shoulders to hold her at a distance.

"No, Nicky, we mustn't. And don't ask me why, because you already know."

"You'll give in to me sooner or later," she said mischievously.

"Only if you get me at a weak moment. Now be a good girl and sit down."

"Aren't I good enough for you?" she asked as she obeyed him. "I know I was only a ladies' maid and –"

"That's got nothing to do with it. I couldn't care less if you swilled out pigs' bins!"

"Then why don't you want to make love to me?"

"Good heavens, Nicky, haven't you any maidenly modesty?"

"None at all," she said so promptly that he laughed.

"I'm glad," he grinned. "I see so much pretence around me that being with someone like you is like breathing fresh air after a fog."

She felt a stab of guilt. No pretence! What would he say when he learned that her entire stay here was a pretence, that everything she had told him was a lie?

The record came to an end and he put on the other side. She longed to feel his arms around her, but knew he would rebuff her if she came near him. Yet remembering how he had kissed her, she felt sanguine about the future.

The second side of the record came to an end and he glanced at his watch and pointed to the door, shaking his head warningly as she went to move towards him.

"If you go on acting like this, Nicky, I'll swear you don't know the facts of life!"

"It's because I do know that I'm acting like this."

"Don't you know how easy it is to arouse a man? If that's what you want –"

"Don't you?"

He looked at her for a long moment in silence. "Heaven help me, but it is," he groaned. "You're the first girl who's

114

stayed here who's — Go to bed," he said in a strangled voice.

"Very well," she said, and with a slight smile left him to his thoughts.

If they were anything like hers, she decided, as she lay in bed, he had several sleepless hours ahead of him. This evening he had made clear much that she had already guessed. Though he had said he did not regard her as a patient, she knew that while she remained in the hostel she would be part of his medical life. Only when she left here would he openly declare his love for her. And he did love her. He was a man with iron control, and for him to have lost it tonight was a declaration without words.

Fleetingly she toyed with the idea of finding a small furnished flat close by. If she moved into it Barnaby would stop seeing her as a patient. Yet she doubted her ability to maintain her pose of being poor once she lived on her own. In the hostel she could occupy herself the whole time, but in furnished rooms it would be another matter, and she could well imagine herself being tempted into shopping along the Kings Road or making a quick dash up to Belgravia to enjoy luxuriating in her own sunken marble bath or sauna room.

How would Barnaby react when he learned her real identity? She had asked herself the question many times and each time had reassured herself with the belief that though he might be annoyed at having been fooled, he would quickly see the amusing side of it. But at this moment she was filled with unease, afraid that he would see her charade as a game she had played to overcome her boredom.

He might be less likely to think this if she had done something worthwhile since leaving school, but she had done nothing except look to the future with blissful innocence and hope that marriage and children would give her all the fulfilment

115

she required. She had quickly realised this was not going to be so. Marriage and children could easily have been come by – there was no shortage of suitors for Nicola Rosten's hand – yet passion without respect was impossible for her, and even short acquaintance with the various men she had believed herself in love with had soon shown her how little they had merited her respect.

She thumped her pillow into a more comfortable position. Looking at her past with a less jaundiced eye she knew she had been partially to blame for her abortive engagements. Even when a man had wanted to control her she had been too head-strong to listen, and none had had the character to insist on being the master for fear of losing her completely. In that respect her wealth had weakened them, and knowing they were in awe of her position had usually been enough to kill her love for them.

But with Barnaby it had been different. Unencumbered by her money, he had seen her solely as a person, and not a person who could give help, but a person who needed it. Nobody had ever seen her in this way before, and she hugged the sensation of being made to believe she was in need of guidance and comfort. When had she realised she had also wanted Barnaby's love? Though the full awareness had come as a revelation to her, she had been intrigued by him from the first moment of meeting. The knowledge of how much he meant to her brought her up from the pillow to sit shivering in bed. It was incredible to think Barnaby held her future happiness in his hands without knowing it. What would she do if he didn't want her – if he found it impossible to accept Nicola Rosten in the same way he had accepted Nicky Rose?

But he had to accept her; she refused to consider any other possibility.

To lull herself back into confidence she thought of the way

116

he had kissed her, relieved every pulsating second of it. Warmth suffused her body and her shivering ceased. I know he loves me, she said to herself, and hugging the thought, drifted into sleep.

CHAPTER TEN

The first time Barnaby had kissed her he had avoided her for several days afterwards, and determined not to let this happen again, Nicola was dressed and in the kitchen by seven o'clock.

Shivering with cold, she put on the kettle, then set out cups and saucers and cut the bread ready for toast. Was Barnaby one of those people who never ate anything in the morning, or did he like a large breakfast? She peered into the ancient fridge which chugged away noisily in one corner of the room, but apart from milk and eggs she saw nothing that would provide a cooked breakfast, and decided to scramble him some eggs.

Some fifteen minutes later she stood outside the door of his bedroom, a brown plastic tray in her arms. Nervously she hesitated, then knocked loudly on the door and went in.

His bed was unoccupied, the blankets flung carelessly aside. From the bathroom came the sound of splashing and she called his name.

The bathroom door flew open and he stood there in his pyjamas, hair tousled, skin still flushed with sleep. "Good lord!" he exclaimed. "What are *you* doing here?"

"I've brought your breakfast."

For the first time he noticed the tray. "I never have breakfast in bed. Take it back to the kitchen."

Anger at him and pity for herself warred within her, but pity won and her eyes filled with tears as she turned to the door and fumbled at the handle. "Could you open it for me?" she mumbled.

Muttering, he came over to her; only then did he see her

tears. "What on earth are you crying for?" Enlightenment dawned. "Not because I asked you to take back my breakfast?"

"I thought you'd enjoy it in bed. Most people do."

"I'm not most people," he said drily. "Look, put it on the table and I'll sit on the bed and have it. Will that make you feel better?"

Her face cleared instantly and she hurried over and set the tray on the bedside table, watching as he kept his promise and sat in front of it. He stared at the scrambled eggs, toast and coffee for so long that she wondered if he was only a black coffee drinker after all, but when he picked up the knife and fork and attacked the food with obvious enjoyment she visibly relaxed.

"You might as well sit down and keep me company while you're here," he said, munching.

Happily she perched on the settee, remembering that she had once slept on it. What a pity she didn't have the opportunity to do so now. The thought brought the colour to her cheeks and the look he flashed her told her that he had guessed her thoughts.

"Not so early in the morning," he grinned. "You've a one-track mind!"

"Only where you're concerned."

He bit into a piece of toast. "You're a minx. Do you know that?"

His teasing attitude told her he was not taking her seriously, and she longed for the time when he could see her as she really was. She glanced down at the skirt and sweater he had brought her.

"You look beautiful," he said, once again divining her thoughts.

"Wait till you see me properly dressed."

"You set too much store by appearances. Haven't you realised yet how unimportant it is?"

"Don't you like your women well dressed?"

"I like *all* women to be well dressed."

"But your particular one," she persisted.

"I don't have a particular one. I love them all."

"You're teasing me again."

"I've decided it's the only way to deal with you."

"When did you decide that?"

"Last night, after you left me."

"After you sent me away, you mean. I didn't want to leave you."

"Oh, Nicky!" He got up from the bed and came over to her. "What am I going to do with you?"

"Let me be part of your life," she said promptly. "I'm not qualified like Joanna, but I'm sure I could help you with your work."

"I bet you could!" He ruffled her hair. "You haven't been very wise in your own young life, but you've sound judgment where other people are concerned. I've listened to you during some of our sessions."

"Do you have any books I can read on the subject? If I knew more I could –"

"I prefer your knowledge the way it is," he interrupted, and tweaked her hair. "You can take the tray away now, but don't repeat it tomorrow morning."

"Don't you like being fussed over?"

"No."

She picked up the tray and went to the door.

"If you've a couple of hours free you can come with me to the hospital," he said unexpectedly. "My secretary has 'flu and I need someone to help me with the patients."

Delighted by the offer, she was nonetheless surprised that

the nurses did not deal with his patients, though she forbore to mention it until they reached the hospital.

"They're my private patients," he said. "And the hospital nurses are on the National Health."

"Then why do you *see* your private patients here?" she asked as they went down a pale green corridor to a small waiting room and slightly larger consulting one.

"Because it's cheaper than Harley Street."

"And you've put all your money into the hostel and can't afford to –"

"Just answer the telephone and save your advice," he retorted. "And don't forget to call me Dr. Grayson while we're here."

"No, Doctor. I mean yes, Doctor."

He smiled and disappeared into the next room as the door behind him opened and his first appointment came in.

If Nicola had needed confirmation of Barnaby's reputation she had it during that morning, for the telephone rang incessantly with people wishing to see him, and a constant stream of patients filled the reception room. Only at lunch time did she have a chance to rest, when she took her lunch in the canteen with the other nurses. They all knew she was deputising for Barnaby's regular secretary and assumed her to be a personal friend of his.

"Joanna Morgan usually helps Dr. Grayson when his secretary's away," one of the more chatty ones said as Nicola sipped her coffee. "This is your first time here, isn't it?"

"Yes. I hadn't realised Dr. Grayson had so many private patients."

"He's been inundated since he became a consultant. If he didn't devote so much time to that hostel of his, he'd be at the top of his tree."

"He is already," Nicola said staunchly.

121

"I was talking about recognition. He won't bother with the right people. You know the sort of thing I mean."

Only too well, Nicola said to herself, but aloud, commented: "I didn't think social climbing was necessary in the medical world."

"It's *always* necessary. But Dr. Grayson doesn't seem to bother. As I said before, all he cares about is that hostel of his."

"Have you ever been there?" Nicola asked.

"No. He doesn't encourage visits. Says he doesn't want the people staying there to feel they're being studied."

"They're not."

"Not in the obvious way, perhaps, but Joanna Morgan's there the whole time, and she's a top psychiatric worker," the nurse grinned. "From the look on your face I can see you don't like her."

"She's not my favourite person," Nicola murmured, and resolutely said no more. Nicola Rosten could be as outspoken as she liked, but Nicky Rose had to be careful. She pushed back her chair. "Work calls," she said lightly, and returned to her office.

The afternoon was as busy as the morning and she was exhausted by the time six o'clock arrived. Not that her own work was particularly hard, merely that her determination not to make any mistakes kept her tense and on edge. But Barnaby appeared as fresh as ever and strode briskly out to the car, enjoining her to hurry up and follow him.

Driving away from the hospital he was laconic with his praise for her help, but the tone of his voice told her he was pleased with her, a fact confirmed when he asked if she would like to help him for a few more days.

Nicola accepted the offer without attempting to hide her pleasure, for she was delighted at the chance of showing him

122

she had the ability to be useful.

For the rest of the week she did her best to take as many chores from him as possible, and though they were rarely alone together – apart from the drive to and from the hospital – she felt she was seeing another side to his character, which not only increased her love for him, but made her doubly frightened of losing him. At the hostel, where everyone called him Barnaby and treated him like a benign older brother, the pretence she was carrying out seemed no more than a prank, but at the hospital, where he was called Dr. Grayson and treated with all the deference that his position entitled him to, the prank seemed childish and stupid, and more than ever she was determined to end it as quickly as she could.

"I don't know how I'd have managed without you," he said to her one evening as they left the hospital. "You've coped marvellously. But I'm sure you'll be delighted to hear that my secretary is coming back tomorrow."

Pleasure was the last thing Nicola felt, and she said so. "I'll loathe staying at the hostel after this. House chores are so boring."

"Not thinking of running away again, are you?"

"What do you mean by 'again'?"

He shrugged, and her anger rose as she realised what he meant.

"I was *not* running off with Marty the other day. I told you I met him by accident."

"I'm sorry," he said instantly. "It's just that somehow you've become –" A child ran into the road and he braked sharply. When he set the car in motion again he did not continue with his sentence and she was forced to guess what he had been going to say.

"Have you never gone out with boys of your own age?" he asked abruptly.

The question caught her unprepared and she thought carefully, knowing it was important to say the right thing. "I've never worried about age. After all, a man of forty can be as callow as one of twenty. And the opposite, of course."

Barnaby kept his eyes on the road. "What made you fall for Marty?"

The impulse to tell him the truth was too strong to be denied and she swivelled round to face him. "There's something I want to tell you. I'm –"

"No," he interrupted swiftly. "Don't tell me anything. I'd no right to question you."

This was a different approach from his previous one and she was not sure she liked it. Yet it followed his earlier assertion that one should think of the future and not the past. But it was not always easy to forget the past, she thought dismally, and wondered what her own reaction would be if she discovered that Barnaby had been involved with someone else – or still was. With Joanna, for instance. Only a few nights ago she had seen them drive off together. Jealousy rose in her like a flood-tide triggering her quick temper.

"It's easy not to ask someone questions if you don't care about them," she snapped. "*I* wouldn't be so casual about you!"

He continued to drive in silence and her anger rose higher. "What about you and Joanna? It's obvious she's in love with you."

"We won't talk about Joanna, if you don't mind." His voice was harder than she had ever heard it. "I respect other people's private life and I expect the same in return."

"People don't have private lives where you're concerned!" she flared. "Look at your group sessions. Everyone tells you *everything*!"

"Only because they want to: not because I ask them."

124

"You never give away anything of *your* thoughts," she went on bitterly, ignoring his remark.

"*I'm* not the one in need of help." His voice was mild again, and he slowed the car down and looked at her. "If you like, I can arrange for you to work at the hospital on a more regular basis. They can always use intelligent assistance."

The change of subject stemmed her temper, but the quick pleasure engendered by his words died as she took in their full meaning.

Guessing her disappointment, he said: "I already have a secretary, Nicky, but if you work in the hospital I'll always call on you if I need extra help myself."

She frowned. Working for Barnaby was one thing; to be at the beck and call of people she did not know was another. Added to which she could not lightly take a job at the hospital and then give it up – which she would have to do once she left the hostel. "I'll think about it," she hedged.

"You needn't take it if you don't want to," he said matter-of-factly. "I merely thought you'd enjoy it."

He drew to a stop outside the hostel, and knowing that once inside she would not be alone with him for the rest of the evening, she was reluctant to leave the car.

"Can we go to the pictures?" The words popped out of their own accord, and his grey eyes crinkled with amusement.

"I'll never be able to follow the way your mind works. What prompted *that* request?"

"I'd like to go out with you," she said truthfully. "I've never been out with a doctor."

"Then we must certainly remedy such a lapse in your education," he said, and before she knew what he was going to do, he put the car in gear and shot off down the road.

"Where are we going?" she gasped, holding on to the eat.

"To the pictures. It's what you wanted, isn't it?"

"Yes, but –"

"If I'd gone in to tell them, I might not have got out again. I'll stop at a phone box and call and say I'll be late."

Anticipating a visit to a local cinema, Nicola was surprised when they sped down the Kings Road to the West End and one of the small theatres showing the latest *avant-garde* film. As she walked into the foyer she knew a momentary apprehension and cast a furtive look round to make sure she could see no one she knew. Happily her luck held, though she did not breathe a final sigh of relief till she had sat down in the darkness of the auditorium.

The film she saw was both witty and wise, but she could not give it her attention, for her whole being was aware of the man beside her who, to her annoyance, seemed totally absorbed in what was being portrayed on the screen.

But once outside the cinema again, he gave her his undivided attention, and tucked her arm through his, striding along the pavement. Continuing the unexpected, he took her to a discothèque, and this time she knew real fear as they went in, for as she took off her coat in the ladies' cloakroom she came face to face with Deborah, the girl whose amorous embrace with Jeffrey had sent her on the flight that had brought Barnaby into her life.

"Nicky!" the girl squealed. "I've been trying to speak to you for weeks, but nobody knew where you were. I wanted to explain about Jeffrey."

"Some other time," Nicola interrupted. "I've someone waiting for me outside."

"But I can't bear having you angry with me. At least let me –"

"It isn't important any more. And I'm not angry with you – I'm delighted. If it hadn't been for you . . ." Nicola stopped

126

and caught Deborah's arm. "Is there anyone else here that I know?"

"Not at the moment. But you know what this place is like. After midnight you'll see *everyone.*"

"We'll be gone long before then."

"Who's the 'we'?" Deborah asked archly. "Do I know him?"

"No. And for heaven's sake pretend you don't know me either."

"Why?"

"It's a joke I'm playing," Nicola said desperately. "I'll call you next week and explain."

Not giving the girl a chance to speak again, she hurried out.

Barnaby was already seated at a table, a plate of smoked salmon sandwiches and a bottle of champagne in front of him.

"Sorry I didn't wait outside for you," he grinned, "but if I hadn't grabbed this table we'd have lost it!" He peered at her. "Why the frown?"

"You shouldn't have ordered champagne. It's so expensive here."

It was the first time she had even given a thought to the money spent on her, and she was surprised at herself. Barnaby seemed surprised too, for he smiled and shrugged.

"So what? I deserve to treat myself to the best! I haven't been out like this for months."

Jealousy rose in her. "Who was the girl last time?"

Ignoring the question, he proffered the sandwiches and she took one and forced herself to eat it, knowing it would anger him if she persisted in her catechism.

Not until they had eaten all the sandwiches and drunk half the champagne did he lead her on to the floor to dance, twirling her around with such abandonment that she was breathless by the time they returned to their table.

"Do you always enter into everything so wholeheartedly?" she gasped.

"If a thing's worth doing, it's worth doing well."

The tempo of the music changed abruptly and the dim lights grew dimmer. Not giving him a chance to sit down, she pulled him back on the floor.

"I thought you were tired," he protested.

"Not for this kind of dancing!"

"This isn't dancing," he said as she clung closely to him. "It's making love in time to music!"

"Is that wrong?" she whispered.

"It's too right," he whispered back, and put his cheek on hers. He had to bend his head a long way down to do so, and she stood on tiptoe and wished she was wearing high heels.

"I'll lift you up if you like," he teased, and proceeded to do so.

"Beast," she said in a low voice, and he chuckled and set her down again, but remained holding her close as the music throbbed soulfully and the vocalist wailed a paean of love.

Nicola could have remained in Barnaby's arms for ever, but a glimpse of Deborah made her realise it was nearly midnight. She had to leave here before any more of her friends arrived. If Jeffrey came in and saw her . . .

She jerked away from Barnaby. "It's late – we must go."

"We don't need to leave on *my* account."

"*I'm* tired," she replied, and at once he led her back to the table.

Within a few moments they were out in the fresh air again, but not until they were some yards from the discothèque did her nervousness decrease and her pace slow down.

"What was all that about?" he asked.

"All what?"

"Your running out of that place like a scalded cat."

The simile made her laugh, and once started the laughter would not stop: a sign of the tension she had been under since entering the discothèque and seeing Deborah.

Catching her arm, Barnaby propelled her towards the car, half-carrying her as her laughter made it progressively difficult for her to walk. He unlocked the door, pushed her into the seat and got in beside her. "Stop it," he commanded. "You'll have hysterics."

"I'm sorry," she giggled, "it must be the champagne." Laughter rose in her again and her lips parted, but before a sound could come his mouth was hard on hers and the laughter died within her, replaced by an urgent longing which he had been the first man to arouse and would be the only man to appease. "Oh, Barnaby," she cried, and clung to him with abandonment.

In the close confines of the car it was not easy for him to push her away, and after a half-hearted attempt to do so, he gave up and instead held her close and stroked her hair and cheeks as though she were a child. With a sigh of contentment she curved herself into his side and rested her head on his shoulder.

"You're just a little girl who likes to be cuddled," he said huskily. "Perhaps you grew up in an orphanage after all, and are still looking for a father-figure."

"I don't feel daughterly towards you."

"I certainly don't feel fatherly!" His voice was still low and relaxed. "You've finally got your way with me, Nicky. This is what you've wanted since you first saw me."

"To have you make love to me?"

"Just to have me, I think. You need the confidence of knowing you're wanted. I suspect it's because you're unsure of

129

yourself as a woman."

She absorbed his words slowly, knowing that on one level they were true; she *was* unsure of herself as a woman. But that was because she had never known whether she was wanted for herself or her money. That was why Barnaby's love meant so much to her. She sighed and clung to him. It was ironic that he could guess her feelings without being aware of the real reason for them.

"Now I've conquered you," she whispered, "what other plans do I have?"

"You haven't conquered me," he replied.

"You're here, aren't you, and you're not pushing me away!"

"I couldn't push you far in this car."

"You're not even trying."

"I know when I'm on a losing bet!" He lifted his head and looked into her eyes, his expression unfathomable in the dimness. "I'm employing different tactics tonight, Nicky. Fighting you will only make you worse, so I'm giving in to you in the hope that you'll be satisfied and . . ."

Deliberately he began to kiss her again, and she wound her arms round his neck and refused to think of what he had just said, happy to accept his surrender without bothering about his motivation.

It was one o'clock when they returned to the hostel and she was dismayed to see Joanna's Renault still parked by the curb.

Even as they walked towards the front door it was opened by Joanna herself, her expression anxious. "Where on earth have you been, Barnaby? I was frantic!"

He snapped his fingers in exasperation. "I tried to call to you once, but the number was engaged, and then it slipped my mind. I'm sorry, my dear."

Joanna forced herself to smile, but she still looked strained. "Where did you go? What happened?"

"I took Nicky to the cinema."

Joanna stared thoughtfully at Nicola's slight figure, and though she did not say a word, her look spoke volumes.

"Go to bed, Nicky," Barnaby intervened. "You look tired."

Sensing that he wanted her to leave, she flashed him a smile and ran up the stairs. At the top of the first flight she turned to wave at him, but the hall was empty and she was just in time to see the door of the sitting room close.

Heart thumping, she leaned over the banisters, but there was no sound from the room below and some of her happiness evaporated. She continued upstairs more slowly, wondering what Joanna was saying to him and, even more important, what he was saying to her.

CHAPTER ELEVEN

Nicola's evening out with Barnaby marked a subtle change in their relationship. There was an ease between them that had not been there before, a camaraderie slightly different from that which he displayed towards the others. However, she did not consider it sufficiently noticeable to cause comment, and she could not hide her surprise when Gillian remarked on it one evening as they got ready for bed.

"We'd have to be blind not to notice it," Gillian said. "Just because most of us are drop-outs it doesn't mean we've got no feelings. Our trouble is that we care too much. That's why so many of us run away." The girl gave her pillow a thump and looked at Nicola. "Loving Barnaby will only bring you trouble. He's interested in you because he wants to know what makes you tick. But don't confuse it with love."

Unwilling to tell Gillian that Barnaby did not consider her to be in need of treatment, and that she was sure his interest was personal, not medical, she turned away without replying.

"I'm not denying he's fond of you," Gillian went on, "but you're still asking for trouble if you go on running after him. He'll never be serious about you."

Nicola climbed into bed. "Let's change the subject."

"Now I've made you angry," Gillian said miserably.

"No, you haven't," Nicky said firmly. "But whatever you say, you won't make me change. Barnaby's the only man I've ever loved."

"What about the other one?" Gillian's thin face was

studiedly indifferent. "The old codger Joanna said she saw you with?"

At no time had Nicola known a greater urge to be truthful. Sharing a room with Gillian she had grown extremely fond of the girl, sensing the gentleness in her that the harsh years of her childhood had not been able to eradicate. Born in a Birmingham slum, with a mother who had not wanted her and a succession of "fathers" who had treated her as a drudge, she had come to Barnaby through the efforts of a probation officer, and had already been at the hostel six months, though she was only now beginning to benefit from it.

"Marty's not my boy-friend," Nicola said carefully. "He's very special in my life, Gillian, but not in that way. One day I'll tell you the whole story."

"There's no need. You know what Barnaby says – your past doesn't matter as long as your present is strong."

"People can't forget their past so easily."

"Who said it was easy?" Gillian reached out and switched off the lamp. "Fall in love with someone else, Nicky. It'll be far better for you."

Nicola thought of this with irony as she watched Barnaby dash through his breakfast the next morning. The kitchen was crammed with people and precedence was given to those who had daily jobs and had to be out of the hostel at a given time. Pouring tea and cutting bread, she thought longingly of the times when she had breakfasted in bed: of the dainty tray with the bone china, the wafer-thin toast and the crisp bacon. But here she was acting waitress at eight o'clock in the morning – and all because of a brown-haired man who treated her most of the time as if she were a child.

"When will you be back tonight, Barnaby?" Frank asked, strolling into the kitchen.

"About seven. It's the end-of-the-month clinic day. That

means I'll be busier than usual."

With a wave of his hand Barnaby went out, and as his steps receded Frank winked at Nicola. "Had to find out how much time we've got to do his room."

"The covers and curtains are made," Gillian said, "and Carole's upstairs putting on the rufflette tape."

"Then we'll get cracking with the paint," Frank replied, directing his glance to the two bearded young men who had just come through the door.

"Not till we've had breakfast," one of them protested.

"Be quick about it, then. And stoke up on tea, because we won't be stopping till lunchtime."

For the rest of the day the activity centred on Barnaby's sitting room, and Nicola enjoyed seeing its metamorphosis. As though by magic the dingy walls were erased by large plastic rollers dipped in pale green paint; the tall windows softened by warm orange drapes and the high ceiling minimised by deep pelmets.

"This little lot must have cost Joanna more than thirty pounds," Frank commented. "She must really be stuck on Barnaby to spend that much."

"She can afford it," Carole said. "Her father's a bank manager and she earns quite a lot herself."

This elicited several comments on the value of a bank manager for a father-in-law, though Nicola paid them little attention, her mind busy with the new facts she had gleaned about Joanna's background. From Gillian she had already learned that Joanna lived with her parents in Harrow, though when the weather was bad she would spend the night at the hostel. She knew too that Barnaby occasionally spent weekends with Joanna's family, and that his mother – now dead – had been at school with Joanna's mother.

"I've a feeling the two mums were hoping for a happy end-

134

ing when they got Joanna to work here," Gillian had expounded. "But if he'd fallen for her, I think he'd have married her by now. It certainly isn't for want of *her* trying!"

These words recurred to Nicola as she watched Carole and Gillian place the new covers on the settee, and she forced them quickly from her mind, saying the first thing that came into her head. "Can't anything be done about that loose spring on the settee?"

"Not without running the risk of the whole thing falling to pieces," Carole answered, tweaking a fold of orange material into place. "We'll order our new lot of furniture from Harrods," she added in pseudo-upper-class tones. "They give better service than the Portobello market — which is where *this* one came from."

Feeling she had been put in her place, Nicola fell silent. The last thing in the world she wanted was to denigrate the effort everyone was making to improve Barnaby's sitting room, and she knew a pang of guilt as she realised how easy it would have been for her to have transformed the room. One phone call would have brought a host of people running who, in a matter of hours, could have turned the room into a Robert Adam bower, a neo-Georgian library or a French Empire drawing-room of magnificent opulence. It required no effort: just money.

Money. The very thought of how it might harm her relationship with Barnaby threatened to destroy the happiness that had filled her since she had woken up this morning. It's ridiculous for me to go on like this, she decided. I must tell him the truth and be done with it. But it was his birthday party this evening and there might not be a chance of catching him alone. Tomorrow at the latest, she vowed, and determined that nothing would dissuade her.

Immediately lunch was finished she set off to meet Marty. It was hard to believe it was already a week since she had seen him, and it was only as she turned the corner of the road that she remembered they had not arranged a specific meeting place. She ran back a few steps to make sure his car was not outside the hostel, but apart from a few vans and a bike the road was empty, and she meandered along the pavement, anticipating every car to be her godfather's. But none stopped, and she turned into the Kings Road and headed for the bookshop.

The assistant recognised her as she came in and went to fetch the book. It had been wrapped in splendid gold paper and he handed it to her with a flourish. "Mr. Martin was in a moment ago enquiring for you," he said. "He asked me to say that if you came in, would you wait here for him."

Nicola breathed a sigh of relief, and resting the book on the counter, stared through the window. She was aware of the young man watching her with curiosity, and knew he was trying to guess her relationship with the upright, handsome man with his clipped moustache and dark hair still only slightly sprinkled with grey. A smile tugged at her lips. In the past few weeks she had seen herself through so many different eyes that she was well aware what picture the assistant had formed.

A blue Rover went slowly past and she waved at its driver, then picked up her package and ran out.

"How's my working girl?" George Martin enquired, smiling at her as she clambered in beside him.

"Still working."

"For how much longer?"

"I'm going to tell Barnaby the truth tonight – if I can."

"Why the doubt?"

"Because it's his birthday and I might not see him alone."

Marty glanced at the package. "You'll be giving him that, I presume?"

"Yes."

"If you're not supposed to have any money how are you supposed to have bought such an expensive book?"

"Oh, lord," groaned Nicola, "I never thought of that. I'll think of something," she added quickly.

"I'm sure you will," her godfather said drily. "You've never disappointed me on that score yet!"

She laughed. "I must have been a dreadful trial to you."

"Why talk in the past? You're not likely to change."

"I'll be Barnaby's responsibility once I'm married to him."

George Martin drew the car to a stop in a quiet turning. "You're very confident he will, aren't you? But then you've never had reason to doubt your ability to get any man you wanted. Being Nicola Rosten has given you an overwhelming choice."

"You're rather belittling my charms," she said, hurt by the remark.

"I'm trying to warn you that Dr. Grayson may not be such a willing pawn as all the other men you've known."

"He loves me. That's why I'm confident." She held out her hand. "Where are all the papers I have to sign?"

Taking the hint, George Martin lifted a briefcase from the back of the car, and for the next hour Nicola was busy perusing a mass of documents and penning her signature to them. Until today she had always signed everything without question, but now she asked several pertinent ones and point-blank refused to sign the last contract handed to her.

"I don't want us to deal with this company," she said, tapping the page with her fingernail. "They underpay their labour and can undercut every other decent firm because of it."

Her godfather looked astonished. "Who told you that?"

"One of the boys at the hostel. He's worked for them."

"In South America?" There was surprise in the clipped voice.

"Frank's been round the world," she replied with a slight smile. "You don't need money to travel if you work your way."

Her godfather gave an exclamation, but she stared at him implacably. "Surely there are other companies we can deal with?"

"Of course. But this price is far below everyone else's."

"It won't affect our profits if we pay a bit more. But when you return the contract I want you to tell them why."

"Is your interest in Rosten affairs temporary or likely to continue?" asked Marty.

"That depends on Barnaby."

Her godfather swallowed, but took the document from her in silence and put it back into his case. "Can we expect you home tomorrow?"

"Providing I manage to talk to Barnaby by then. But I'll make it as quick as I can." She half-turned and clutched Marty's arm. "I suddenly feel frightened. What do you think he'll say when he finds out?"

George Martin hesitated. Never one to lie to her, he was obviously not going to do so now. "I don't know him, my dear, so I can't say. But if he loves you – as you tell me he does – I'm sure things will work out."

"I hope so," she gulped, and with a little sob flung her arms round his neck, hugged him and then opened the car door, this time careful to make sure there was no white Renault in sight.

Holding the large package against her chest, Nicola hurried into the hostel and up to her room. Carefully she slid it under the eiderdown on her bed, knowing it would remain there undetected until she gave it to Barnaby later that evening. What

138

a pity she had not told him the truth about herself before tonight. Had she done so they could have spent his birthday in more luxurious surroundings: a celebration party that could also have served to introduce him to her friends, or a quiet dinner *à deux* in a penthouse restaurant that gave a breathtaking view of London. But because the truth had not been told she and Barnaby must celebrate his birthday with strong tea, weak coffee and shop-bought pastry.

Barnaby returned from the hospital later than usual. From the basement window of the kitchen his car could be heard gliding to a stop outside the front gate, and silently everyone trooped to the bottom of the stairs and listened as he entered the hall and cross the floor to his sitting room.

"I wish I could see his face when he goes in," Frank whispered.

"I wonder if he'll notice the curtains," Carole muttered.

There was the sound of a door opening, and a loud exclamation followed by a long silence.

No one breathed, no one stirred, and looking round her at the upturned anxious faces Nicola was touched in a way she had never expected. These young people genuinely cared for Barnaby, she thought tremulously, and felt her eyes blur with tears. But they had no chance to spill, for there came a sudden shout and then the clatter of steps as Barnaby rushed down the stairs.

Everyone except Nicola ran forward to greet him, shouting congratulations as well as telling him what particular part they had played in transforming his sitting room. Watching his face, she realised how moved he was, and sensed what it meant to him to know he was the centre of such a spontaneous show of affection. Above the crowd pressing in on him their eyes met, and warmth flooded through her as though his very look was a touch.

Dinner was more rowdy than usual, for though the food was still the ubiquitous stew, Barnaby produced several bottles of wine. It was not inexpensive Spanish as she had expected, but a pleasant French one with a good bouquet. How typical and generous it was of him, she thought. Another person might well have been satisfied to produce an indifferent wine, knowing that even the cheapest one would have been accepted with pleasure. Yet he had bought a good vintage; not sufficiently expensive to be obvious, but dear enough to show that he regarded tonight as an occasion he was sharing with friends and not patients who were dependent on him medically and financially.

Joanna was seated on Barnaby's right. Whenever she stayed for a meal she always took her place next to him as though it were hers by right, as indeed it was if one dined in order of precedence, Nicola conceded, and wondered what Joanna would have said if she had seen her and Barnaby in the car the night before.

Looking up, she saw the hard brown gaze fixed on her. There was a triumphant look in them that sent a chill through her body, as though Joanna was hiding something exciting. Nicola's heart pounded as she pondered its cause.

"You're not drinking your wine." Barnaby spoke to Nicola directly for the first time that evening.

With a guilty start she picked up the thick glass and sipped. "You can do better than that," he encouraged. "Drink it up and have some more."

"It will make me drunk."

"I doubt it. It will just relax you."

"Perhaps Nicky doesn't want to relax," Joanna put in.

"Why not?" Barnaby smiled.

"Because it's too easy to give yourself away then."

"I don't think Nicky's hiding any secrets."

140

"You'd be surprised." Joanna's eyes slid to Nicola again. "Isn't that so?"

"All women have secrets," Nicola smiled, marvelling at the quickness of her own response. "Mystery adds to our attraction."

"I hate mysteries," Frank interposed, joining the conversation. "I like everything to be above board."

"So does Barnaby," Joanna said.

Nicola stared at her wine glass, chiding herself for being frightened by Joanna's remarks. It was only the guilt she felt at hiding her identity that made her read more into the remark than was meant. Joanna could have no idea who she really was.

All at once Barnaby pushed back his chair and stood up. Everyone stopped speaking and he smiled at the silent faces. "I haven't commanded such attention for weeks," he said in mock seriousness. "So I'd better use it to good advantage and say that you've done a magnificent job on my sitting room. It's worthy of a full colour page in *House and Garden*!"

"Joanna planned it," Frank said, "*and* found the cash. We only did the work."

"I wouldn't use the word 'only'," Barnaby replied gravely. "It was a great effort. Beats me how you managed to get it done in the time." He glanced at Carole. "I take it it was you who did the covers?"

"And Gillian," Carole replied, flushing happily. "All the others were busy with the painting."

"Except Nicky," Joanna murmured, and looked her full in the face. "You weren't here this afternoon, were you?"

All eyes turned on Nicola and she turned scarlet.

"Let's clear the dishes," Carole said roughly, and she and Gillian noisily stood up.

Everyone else took the hint and there was a general movement as the table was cleared, wine bottles removed and dishes stacked in the sink ready to be washed.

"We've some sandwiches and cocoa for later," Tom said to Barnaby. Since his last epileptic attack he had been confined to bed and this was his first evening down.

"If you could stay out of the living room for half an hour it would give us time to get things ready."

"I like the way you take it for granted we aren't going to have our usual discussion tonight," Barnaby said in tones of mock disapproval.

"We thought we'd give you the evening off!" Tom grinned.

"Is that a treat for me or for you?" Barnaby grinned back as he went to the door. "Still, I can take a hint that I'm not wanted. I'll relax in my new sitting room till you let me join you again!"

"Be careful not to brush against the door or the walls," Frank warned. "The paint might still be tacky."

Barnaby nodded and glanced to where Nicola was standing. Then his eyes moved to Joanna before returning again to her. "I'll see you upstairs, then," he said, and went out.

Surreptitiously Nicola glanced at Joanna. The girl was in conversation with a red-bearded boy who had arrived at the hostel only the day before. Nicola wondered whether she would have time to go up and give Barnaby his present now. If she delayed doing so she might not get another chance of being alone with him.

Quietly she slipped out and ran up to her room. The package was where she had left it and she lifted it out and looked at it, then she set it down and went to the cracked mirror to comb her hair. Excitement had lent colour to her pale skin and a bright sparkle to her eyes, so that they looked more green than grey. Her mouth seemed redder and fuller too, though that was probably because nervous tension had made her bite her lips throughout the evening.

Picking up the package, she returned to the hall and, without giving herself time to think, knocked on the door of the sitting room and went in. Barnaby was in an armchair by the fire, but at the sight of her he got slowly to his feet, though he made no move to come nearer.

"I – I want to give you this," she stammered, and held out the package.

He looked at it and one shaggy brow lifted. "It looks nearly as big as you!"

"It's heavy," she said. "Take it."

He did so, and with quick precise movements unwrapped the paper to disclose the book.

Nicola watched him in a fever of anxiety, her heart hammering so loudly that she could not hear any other sound except its beat. It was ridiculous to be so nervous about the giving of a present. Even if it was not what he wanted it would surely meet with his approval. But he said nothing and looked at the book as though he had never seen one before in his life. Unable to bear the suspense, she ran over to his side. "Isn't it what you want? I thought you liked Gauguin. Those paintings you have in your bedroom – they're in the same sort of colours, and I thought –"

"It's a magnificent book," he said quickly. "But I –" He stopped and cleared his throat. "I never expected anything like it." He turned several of the pages reverently. "It's almost as good as looking at the real paintings. I've never seen such wonderful reproductions."

"It's a special edition," she explained.

Silent again, he continued to riffle through the pages, and she watched him, puzzled by his expression. There was no doubt that he was pleased, but it was not pleasure alone that marked his face, and she waited nervously for him to speak, half-anticipating what he would say and completely ready with her answer. Pray God he would see the funny side to her impersonation and not be angry with her.

"You shouldn't have bought me such an expensive present," he murmured at last. "I'd have appreciated anything from you Nicky, no matter how little its value."

"But I wanted to give you this." About to say she could afford it, she stopped, for even in her own ears the words sounded spoiled. What was the best way of telling him the truth? She had rehearsed it many times, but now that the moment had come all her carefully worked out phrases had disappeared, and all she could think of was her longing to throw herself into his arms. "The cost doesn't matter," she continued desperately, "as long as you like it."

"It's wonderful," he said firmly. "But it *is* expensive. I hope you didn't do anything foolish in order to get it for me."

"Not unless you consider it foolish of Nicky to return to her old way of life," a hard clear voice interrupted them.

With a gasp Nicola swung round to see Joanna.

"I assume there's a meaning behind that remark," Barnaby said.

"There certainly is," Joanna retorted. "And you're not going to like it."

"*I'll* tell Barnaby the truth," Nicola interrupted. "I was just going to when you came in."

"Pity I didn't give you a few minutes longer, then. It might have been amusing to know what story you'd made up this time! You've never been short on lies, have you?"

"For goodness' sake, Joanna," Barnaby exploded, "tell me what's on your mind."

"Nicky's playing you for a fool. *That's* what's on my mind! I know where she bought that book and how she got the money for it. From that man Marty – the one she promised

144

you last week she was never going to see again."

Nicola stared at Joanna, repelled by the venom in her voice, yet at the same time curious to know how she had discovered the truth; but not the whole truth, she amended, smiling slightly, for Joanna still believed Marty was her elderly protector.

"Look at the way she's laughing," Joanna said harshly.

"I'm not laughing," Nicola said. "I merely find your bitchiness amusing."

"*I* don't find it amusing." Barnaby spoke to Nicola directly for the first time since Joanna had burst in on them. "Is what Joanna said the truth?"

"In a way," Nicola replied. "Marty *did* give me the money."

"Last week you promised me you wouldn't see him again."

"I had a reason for saying that. Please, Barnaby, let me talk to you alone."

"There's no point," he said harshly. "What you want to say can just as easily be said in front of Joanna."

"I want to talk to you alone," she repeated. "Please, Barnaby."

"Please, Barnaby," Joanna mocked, and moved close to him. "Don't tell me you're going to fall for that again. She's already made a fool of you once!" Joanna turned on Nicola. "You'll need a lot more than lies to get you out of trouble now. Your little game is over; though it beats me why you even bothered to play it. I saw your boy-friend in the bookshop this afternoon. I went there to pick up a print I'd ordered and he came in and asked if the book he'd paid for last week had been collected yet."

Before Nicola could reply Joanna swung back to Barnaby. "Don't you see what she did? She got money from one man to make a play for another! That's why she arranged to meet him last week — to get him to buy the book for her."

"Did he buy the book for you, Nicky?" Barnaby asked.

"Please let me talk to you alone," she cried.

"Just answer me," he grated. "Did this man buy the book for you?"

"Yes, but —"

"Then you can take it back to him." In a violent gesture he sent the book crashing to the floor.

"Barnaby, don't! You don't understand." She ran over and put her hand on his arm, but he flung it away with such force that she staggered back.

"I understand only too well," he shouted. "For some reason best known to yourself you have to conquer every man you meet, no matter who he is or how old he is. It's part of your sickness, Nicky, but I thought I could help you work your way through it."

"You can!" she cried. "I mean, it isn't true. Barnaby, please, you've got to listen to me!"

"I'm finished listening to you. I don't ever want to hear you or see you again. Get out of the hostel, Nicky. We've no room here for you." He strode out, slamming the door so hard that the curtains trembled on their hooks.

Nicola drew a shuddering breath. What an ugly and unnecessary scene this had been; ugly because of all that Joanna had implied, and unnecessary because if Joanna had come in only a few moments later the whole truth would already have been disclosed. Not that any lasting harm had been done, she would merely be unable to tell Barnaby the truth in the light-hearted way she had planned. She would have to go in search of him and begin her story knowing that he was full of anger towards her. Yet how quickly his anger would die when he learned the whole story.

146

She took a step forward and found her way barred by Joanna.

"I hope you're going upstairs to pack?"

"I'm going to see Barnaby first."

"You're wasting your time. Your lies won't help you now. You're a little tramp, Nicky, and Barnaby knows it!"

"You'd better be careful what you say," Nicola said tightly.

"You're the one who should be careful. Do you think I haven't seen the game you've been playing? You set your cap at Barnaby the minute you got here."

"And I've got him," Nicola flared, anger destroying her discretion. "You've done everything you can to turn him against me, but you haven't been able to stop him loving me."

"Loving you!" Joanna taunted, and burst out laughing. " 'Wanting' is the word I'd use! That's the only emotion you're capable of arousing in a man. Not that it seems to worry you."

"You really do hate me, don't you?" Nicola said slowly. "I suppose it's because *you* love Barnaby too."

"If you're implying I'm jealous . . ." Colour flooded into Joanna's face, suffusing her usually placid features with a pink glow. "The most difficult part about having you here was watching you make a play for Barnaby and not being able to tell you the truth. But he wouldn't let me. He knew how you felt about him and he was sure he could help you to work your way out of it."

"Work my way out of it?" Nicola echoed. "What's that supposed to mean?"

Joanna sighed heavily. "Lots of the girls Barnaby tries to help fall in love with him. They're immature and emotionally stunted — that's generally why they're here — and they see him as their saviour. But once they start to make something of their lives they realise that what they felt for him was part of their growing up."

"*I* was already grown up when I met Barnaby," Nicola said coldly.

"In years, perhaps. Not in terms of maturity." Joanna was fully in command of herself now and spoke with calm authority. "You were a child, Nicky. Those are Barnaby's words, not mine."

"He didn't kiss me as if I were a child," Nicola tossed her head in anger.

"He found that the most difficult part of the whole thing. Your physical wantonness and your – your childlike trust in him. Any man, other than Barnaby, would have taken advantage of it. You can count yourself lucky you came up against someone as ethical as him. Though even *he* found it hard to keep you at arm's length the whole time."

"If you're trying to make me regret loving Barnaby you're not succeeding. If you'd kindly get out of my way I'd like to go and talk to him."

Joanna did not move. Her skin was still pink and there was a strange glitter in her eyes. But it was her hands that caught Nicola's attention, for the blunt fingers twined and intertwined with each other, showing an uncertainty that was not to be seen on her face. "It won't do you any good, Nicky." Her voice was unexpectedly husky. "I can see I'll have to tell you the whole truth. Barnaby didn't want anyone to know because . . . well, he hates a fuss and, more important still, he feels it might affect some of the girls here – but you'll be leaving here tonight anyway, so it won't make any difference if I tell you."

"Tell me what?"

"About Barnaby and myself. At least it will help you to

understand why I was angry at the way you tried to monopolise him. I know you thought I was petty about it, but –" she shrugged – "I may be a qualified social worker, but when it comes to love I'm as jealous and possessive as most women."

Nicola's heart thumped heavily. "What are you trying to say?"

"Can't you guess? Barnaby and I are engaged. We're planning to be married in a couple of months."

"No," Nicola gasped. "I don't believe it!" She stared at Joanna and the brown eyes returned her gaze without wavering.

"It's true," Joanna said quietly. "You can ask Barnaby yourself if you don't believe me. He tried to tell you the night he took you to the pictures – but I gather things got a bit out of hand. You made your feelings so clear that he was afraid you'd run away if he told you the truth."

"And now?"

"You're leaving anyway. This man Marty obviously has a strong hold over you, and perhaps if you play your cards right he might marry you. He's much older than you, of course, but that might be what you need."

Nicola still could not speak and Joanna moved a step closer, her face warm with compassion. "Right now you think you love Barnaby, but I can assure you that once you go back to your friend you'll forget the hostel and everyone in it. Barnaby has such a strong personality that –"

"Stop it!" Nicola cried, and blindly walked to the door. Her hands were fumbling on the knob when Joanna came to stand beside her.

"You'll get over it, Nicky. All the other girls have. If you'd like to leave the hostel tonight I can take you in my car."

"That won't be necessary." Nicola spoke with difficulty, her mouth so dry that her tongue could barely move. "I've nothing to pack."

"Barnaby bought you a couple of dresses. I'm sure he'd want you to take them."

"Leave them for another homeless stray. I won't need them any more."

"Is it back to your old life, then?"

"Naturally! It's what you thought I'd do all along, isn't it?" Not waiting for an answer, Nicola ran out.

Without bothering to fetch a coat she wrenched open the front door and raced down the path and along the pavement. The air struck cold against her bare arms, but it did not deter her, so anxious was she to put the hostel as far behind her as she could.

So much for all her dreams and hopes. What a fool she had been not to see the reality of the situation instead of her own projection of it! Despite Barnaby's insistence that everyone call him by his first name, he was and always had been a doctor in charge of a social experiment, with everyone at the hostel a part of it. But stupidly she had believed he had seen her as a woman, had read into everything he had said a personal meaning which had never been there.

Of course he had responded to her. She had never given him a chance not to! From the moment they had met she had flung herself at him. Wanton, Joanna had called her behaviour, and wanton she had undoubtedly been.

But she had loved him and hadn't cared if he had known it. Tears filled her eyes at the thought. How much heartache she would have been saved if he had been equally truthful with her. Despite the psychological reasons Joanna had given her for Barnaby's secrecy over his engagement, Nicola could not condone his behaviour. He had known she wanted him and he had deliberately allowed her to believe that only the fact that she was staying in the hostel under his care was preventing him from openly declaring his own love for her. Yet how skilfully he had shown her his feelings without putting them into words. Remembering his kisses and the touch of his hands on her body, she burned with shame. Even Joanna knew he had responded to her, for guilt must have made him tell her so.

The glare of headlamps pierced the darkness and she shrank back against a fence. If this was Barnaby coming in search of her she had no intention of being found. If she saw him now she would break down; humiliate herself more by letting him know she still cared for him. But the lights were those of a taxi, and as it came abreast of her she saw it was unoccupied, and ran forward to stop it.

"Belgravia," she said, opening the door and jumping in. "I'll direct you once we get there."

The cab jerked into motion, each chug of its engine taking Nicola further from the hostel. Yet no matter what physical distance separated her from Barnaby Grayson she knew that for a long time to come he would be heartbreakingly alive in her heart.

CHAPTER TWELVE

"How much longer is it going to take you to get Dr. Grayson out of your system?" George Martin posed the question to his goddaughter one afternoon early in March, six weeks after she had left the hostel. "It never took you this long before."

"I was never in love before."

"Are you sure it isn't a question of wanting something because you can't have it?"

She sighed and turned away, then heard him walk across the carpet to stand beside her as she looked out over the quiet square. "Forgive me, Nicola. I shouldn't have said that."

"I don't blame you for thinking it. I even wonder myself if that's the reason. I wish it was."

"It isn't, is it?" George Martin said. "You really did love him."

"I do," she corrected, "but I'll get over it in time. I've got to," she muttered. "It can't always hurt like this."

"Why not go to America? I know the Campbells have invited you."

"Running away won't help."

"Nor will burning the candle at both ends. All that'll do is burn you out." He put his hands on her shoulders and turned her round, looking concerned as he felt the brittleness of her bones.

Always slight and delicate in appearance, she now looked ethereal, as though a strong wind could blow her away. He sighed, wondering if the glitter and the gaiety that was so much a part of the girl he loved like a daughter would ever return.

He touched his fingers to her hollow cheek. "Even make-up can't hide the shadows under those big eyes of yours," he warned. "You can't go on like this, my dear. Grayson's in love with another girl and you must forget him."

"Don't you think I'm trying?" she cried, and pulling out of his grasp, walked with quick nervous steps around the room, an elfin figure of a girl with a pale, heart-shaped face and dark, flyaway hair. Silk skirts rustled round her silk-clad legs, and expensive perfume lingered in the air as she moved. What a far cry she was from the girl who had entered the hostel and found a new world she had never dreamed of. But that was in the past, and her future now was a bleak one; rich with money but poor of love – at least the love of the one and only man she wanted.

For the first few hours after her return home Nicola had lived in the hope and dread of Barnaby coming in search of her, and only as day dawned did she realise he still did not know her identity. He believed she had once worked for Nicola Rosten and had stolen her mink wrap, therefore this would be the last place he would expect to find her. Yet even if he had found her it would have served no purpose. No matter from how many different angles she looked at the situation, she still could not condone his behaviour. It had been wrong of him not to tell her about Joanna. Wrong and cruel.

The knowledge that she had been able to rouse him to passion no longer gave her the same satisfaction that it had done a month ago, for distance made her see things more clearly and she was able to see her actions through his eyes, and guess the pity he must have felt for the girl he had believed her to be. Nicky Rose, trying to escape from a relationship with a man old enough to be her father – a girl who had said she had never been able to love boys her own age. Yet in encouraging her to love him what had Barnaby hoped to achieve? And for how

153

long had he intended keeping his engagement to Joanna a secret? The questions multiplied with such rapidity that she had forced herself to stop thinking of them. Unless she did, she would go mad.

"The car's here," Marty said behind her. "Did you mean it about coming to the office with me?"

"Of course." She picked up a sable coat lying on the back of a chair and negligently slung it around her shoulders. "Don't you think I'm learning the business fast?"

"Too fast," he smiled. "But then you've a Rosten head on your shoulders."

Sitting in the back of the Rolls George Martin gave her a brief outline of the meeting they were going to attend, and by the time the vast edifice of Rosten's London headquarters in Cheapside came into view, Nicola was fully acquainted with the details of the bid her company was going to make for another. Not that it would matter if they didn't succeed, she thought with a sigh. What was the worth of one million when one had so many already? It was only possible to eat one meal at a time and drive in one car at a time, she thought ironically, and even with two arms and ten fingers there was a limit to the diamonds you could wear. It was even pointless to buy more houses, for no matter where she lived, there was only one place she cared about: the hostel where she had met and fallen in love with Barnaby. The hostel where he might even now be living as Joanna's husband.

Memory of the hostel lay heavy within her like undigested food. It had epitomised the happiest and also the saddest time in her life, and the thought of it seemed destined to remain with her for ever. It was depressing knowledge and she wondered bleakly how she was going to cope with the years ahead of her. Would every house she lived in remind her of the large and shabby one near the Embankment? Would a green-painted wall awaken memory of a sitting room that had witnessed her first real kiss of love, and would she always sit in a settee and wait for a spring to stab her flesh, the way thoughts of Barnaby kept stabbing her heart?

Perhaps if there were more hostels she would stop thinking about one particular one. The idea blossomed so quickly that she knew it must have lain in her subconscious almost from the time she had returned to Belgravia, and when she mentioned it to Marty over dinner that evening it had already burgeoned into full, flowering life.

"I intend forming a charitable trust to open a dozen hostels," she said.

"Indeed," George Martin replied with commendable lack of surprise.

"Yes. I'm going to call it Rosten Homes. It will set up hostels in all the major cities in Great Britain."

"A worthy thing to do." George Martin still spoke without expression.

"You know why I'm doing it," she retorted.

"Ah! I wondered if you were prepared to admit it."

"Of course I'll admit it. I intend putting Barnaby in charge of running them."

"I see. If you can't have your doctor one way you're determined to have him another." In the glow of the candlelight from the silver candelabra George Martin's face looked infinitely sad. "If you're doing this in the hope that Grayson will break his engagement . . ."

"That idea was *not* in my mind." Nicola's voice was ice-cold though her body burned as though with fever. "And I wouldn't have him if he came crawling to me on his knees! He made a fool of me, Marty, and —" she clenched her hands — "we Rostens don't like being made fools of."

"*You* made a fool of him too. You pretended to be destitute and —"

"I didn't pretend about being in love with him — the way he did with me! He knew I meant what I said — that I wanted him — that I'd have given him anything he asked for." She pushed back her chair and went to stand by the fireplace. "He had no right to lead me on," she cried. "He should have told me the truth about Joanna."

"I understood from what Miss Morgan said to you that having you dependent on him was part of his treatment. It was his way of breaking your dependence on the old man you were supposed to be running away from."

"Joanna only said that to try and whitewash him. He *never* regarded me as a patient. He told me so himself."

"Nonetheless you were staying at the hostel."

"Only as a place to live," she said dully. "He knew I remained there because of him, and he encouraged me. That's why I can't forgive him."

"Perhaps he *was* attracted to you," George Martin murmured. "You can't blame him for that."

"He's a doctor — he should know that —"

"You just said he wasn't treating you in his capacity as a doctor. Be fair, Nicola."

"He wasn't fair to me," she flared, "and he's going to pay for it."

"By having to be grateful to you for the new hostels? He'll never accept the job from you on that basis. Never."

"He won't know I'm behind the scheme until he's agreed to run it. Don't forget he still thinks I'm Nicky Rose. By the time he learns who I really am he'll be too deeply involved to back out."

"I wouldn't bank on that," her godfather replied. "From

what you've told me of him I'd say he's a pretty obstinate man."

"He wants to open more hostels, Marty. It's the biggest ambition of his life. He'll never turn down the chance, no matter what it costs him in personal pride. Even having to report to me each month won't stop him from —"

"I thought you had a particular catch in it for him," George Martin intervened, leaning back in his chair and looking her full in the face.

"Do you blame me?" She met his gaze defiantly. "He'll have to dine with Nicola Rosten once a month to keep her up to date with everything that's going on." Her mouth curved in a hard smile. "He's going to feel pretty small every month, isn't he?"

"Yes," her godfather agreed. "But so, my dear, will you."

Nicola remembered these words many times during the next few weeks, but she refused to recognise the truth of them, nor would she allow them to dissuade her from her plans.

Long tedious hours with an army of lawyers finally established the Rosten Homes Trust, whose money was to come from the main charitable foundation set up by her father many years before. Never had Nicola been so glad of being an heiress as she was at this moment. Money had not been able to give her the man she loved, but it would at least keep him within the orbit of her life, and if happiness came from making that man eat humble pie then she would be happy indeed.

Again and again she visualised their next meeting, when he would come into the room expecting to see Nicola Rosten and find himself face to face with Nicky Rose. What a far cry it was from the way she had originally planned to tell him the truth on the night of his birthday. But she must not think of that; to do so would weaken her resolve and make her concede

157

that Marty was right. But Marty wasn't right. It wouldn't hurt her to watch Barnaby squirm at her dinner table once a month, nor would it hurt her to know she was forcing him to treat her with a respect he had never shown towards poor Nicky Rose. And what about Joanna? How would she react at knowing her husband was dining *tête-à-tête* with the girl she had once so cruelly dismissed as being no better than a tramp? Oh no, Nicola thought to herself, she wasn't going to regret what she was doing. She was going to enjoy every minute of it.

Determined to keep her identity a secret until the very moment when Barnaby entered her home, Nicola left her godfather to make all the arrangements with him – from making the telephone call that set up the first meeting to tell him about Rosten Homes, to the final one where the documents were presented for him to sign, thereby making him chief executive of the scheme. Only then did Nicola's tension ease and triumph override all other emotion.

Aware of this, George Martin could not hide his disquiet. "Forget your monthly meetings with Grayson," he advised. "He's a strong character, Nicola, and you'll hurt yourself far more than him."

"It'll hurt him too," she retorted. "He won't like eating humble pie."

"Are you sure he knew you loved him?" her godfather persisted. "I must say he doesn't strike me as the sort of man who'd encourage a girl, particularly someone he was trying to help."

"He encouraged me all right," she said bitterly.

"Wasn't it the other way around? You're a lovely girl, Nicola, you'd go to most men's heads."

Angrily she stood up and increased the volume of sound coming through the stereo, deliberately making further conversation impossible.

Accepting defeat, her godfather fell silent, and the subject was not referred to again. In the days that followed Nicola had to force herself to be patient. She longed to confront Barnaby with the truth of the situation but knew she must refrain from doing so until he had become too deeply involved in the scheme to give it up.

Because it was becoming increasingly harder to stay in London without being tempted to drive to Chelsea and catch a glimpse of him, she accepted an invitation to stay with friends in America, and determinedly whiled away several weeks in Palm Springs, a month on a ranch in Arizona and several more weeks in Kentucky, where the lush green grass had nothing in common with the grey concrete of the Embankment, and her antique fourposter bed was nothing like the narrow divan on which she had once spent the night.

It was the end of May before she returned to England, met at the airport by her always devoted godfather and whisked along the busy motorway — how small it was compared with the American version — to the comfort of her own home.

"It's so good to be back," she cried when, having greeted the servants, she stood in the drawing-room and looked around her.

"I was beginning to wonder if you intended to return," George Martin remarked. "I hear Stephen Campbell was keen to make you stay in New York."

"He asked me to marry him."

"And?"

"And I said no, thank you." She spun round on her heel, lovely and graceful as ever and no longer as bone-shakingly thin. "What's happening with Barnaby?"

"I was hoping you'd forgotten."

"You know me better than that."

Her godfather sighed. "Dr. Grayson is working full time on

159

the scheme. Seven of the twelve houses are already open and the others are nearing completion."

"Why the delay? He's got the money to get all the staff he wants."

"Some of the houses needed altering. That's where the delay has been. There's no problem about staffing them. Grayson has an excellent reputation and psychologists are more than anxious to work with him."

"Where is he now?" she asked.

"In Liverpool. Two new homes have opened there. He's then going on to Glasgow."

"Let me know when he's in London. We must begin our monthly dinners."

"Are you still determined to go through with that childish idea?"

"That childish idea," Nicola retorted, "was the whole purpose of the scheme. I don't want you to refer to it any more. It's a small price for Barnaby to pay to get all his ambitions realised in one go."

"It's not what *he'll* have to pay that worries me," George Martin replied. "It's what it's going to cost *you*."

Angrily she swung away from him. Her hip knocked against a side table and the telephone standing on it tingled in protest. Shaken that the thought of Barnaby could still bring her to the point of tears, she lifted the receiver and without giving herself time to think, dialled Jeffrey Simonds' number.

"Jeffrey," she said gaily, as his voice came on the line. "It's Nicola. I've just returned from the States. I'm free tonight if you ... Fine. Pick me up at eight." She put the telephone down on his stammering delight and pushed away the distaste she felt at being able to command him so easily. Not a word from her since the night of Deborah's party, yet he had fallen over himself to play lapdog to her again; or was she doing him an injustice? Perhaps he still felt so conscience-stricken at having been caught making love to another girl that he was willing to do anything to make amends?

When he called for her later that evening he seemed more than eager to begin where they had left off, and gave her a well-rehearsed apology for the tawdry scene she had witnessed, as well as a reiteration of his love and devotion for the future.

"Don't let's talk about the future." She flashed him a brilliant smile. "Let's play things by ear and see what happens."

"But I love you, Nicola. I always have. You're the most wonderful girl in the world."

"And one of the richest!"

He reddened. "Your humour hasn't changed."

"I'm sorry," she said without contrition, "but you can't expect to begin where we left off."

"I'm delighted you're letting me begin at all." With a graceful gesture he drew her hand to his lips, and then led her out to his car.

For the next few weeks he was her constant escort, but being with him again showed her more clearly than ever that it was impossible for her to turn back the clock. She recognised Jeffrey's charm and good looks, she appreciated his wit and quick – though facile – mind, but she knew she would never be able to accept him as a husband. But then at the moment the thought of any man other than Barnaby was anathema. One day she might be able to consider marriage – not because she would ever love a man as much as she loved Barnaby but because she knew she did not possess the strength of mind to face years of loneliness.

It was incredible that Barnaby had come to mean so much to her in so short a time. Was it because he had been the first man to see her as a woman and not as a bank balance? That was the obvious reason; though the less obvious one was that she had been drawn to his strength and compassionate understanding of others; that she had recognised in him a human being ready to offer help without thought of return; who gave himself without need of recompense. Only with her had he betrayed himself, for her childlike appeal had weakened his strength and passion had overcome compassion. But was this reason enough to humiliate him? Obstinacy prevented her from answering the question, and whenever it returned to mock her she resolutely pushed it away. She had made a decision and she would stick by it.

A fortnight after her return to England her godfather told her that Barnaby had returned to London.

"He's extremely anxious to meet Nicola Rosten," he said drily. "He wants to thank her for all she's done."

"He wrote to me," she shrugged. "But I never replied."

"When do you want to have the dinner?"

"As soon as possible."

"Do you wish to invite Miss Morgan? He might be married by now."

"Haven't you asked him?"

"I'm not supposed to know about her." He hesitated. "Would you like me to find out?"

"No," Nicola said sharply. "I don't want her here even if she *is* his wife."

"I wish you'd abandon the idea."

"Well, I won't. So go ahead and fix it up."

The next morning her godfather telephoned to say the dinner party was arranged for that night. "I thought we'd get it over as quickly as possible. You'll be like a bear with a sore head until we do."

At seven o'clock that evening Nicola looked at the mound of dresses lying on her bed and decided she didn't have a thing to wear.

"But all your clothes are new," Maria exclaimed, throwing her hands up to heaven. "Mademoiselle looks beautiful in all of them." She picked up a red taffeta. "In this you look like a devil, and in this one –" she pointed to a green chiffon – "like a sea-nymph."

"I think it's more appropriate that I look like a good fairy," Nicola said abruptly, and crossing to the wardrobe drew out a dress she had not worn for a long time.

"Why *a* good fairy?" Maria asked.

"Because Cinderella found one."

Aware of Maria looking at her curiously, Nicola stopped talking and began to dress, refusing to let her nerves get the better of her and keeping her mind a blank as to what the next few hours would hold.

Finally dressed to go downstairs, she stood in the centre of the room and wished she could be transported to Mars – to anywhere that would take her out of Barnaby's orbit. But it was too late now. She picked up her silver handbag and went sedately down the stairs.

Only in the hall did she pause to look at herself in the gilt mirror on a wall above a French console table. How different she was from Nicky Rose! No one would mistake her for a waif tonight. The finest of French lace, thin as a cobweb and the same silver grey, clung to every line of her figure. It was patterned with iridescent bugles so that she seemed to be wearing a shimmer of light from which the pearly pink of her shoulders rose to support the graceful column of her neck. Lavish but carefully-applied make-up accentuated the fullness of her mouth and her large eyes, whose thick curling lashes could not quite disguise the haunted look in the grey-green depths. Her long dark hair was caught away from her face by a glitter of diamond combs, and fell into thick ringlets on the

163

nape of her neck, moving provocatively every time she turned her head.

From the street came the sound of a car. There was something familiar about its engine and her heart hammered against her ribs. Hurriedly she entered the drawing-room where her godfather was waiting.

"Dressed for the kill," he said lightly, and handed her a glass of champagne. "No point waiting for our guest. You look as if you can do with this right now."

"I think he's here already," she said, and at that moment heard the front door close. Liquid spilled on to her hand and she set down the goblet on the table beside her. Behind her she heard the drawing-room door open and the butler announce Barnaby by name.

All emotion in Nicola seemed suspended, and as though she were a puppet manipulated by an unseen hand, she turned to face the man who had just come in. Taller and broader than she had remembered and looking unfamiliar in a well-cut dinner jacket, he was as different from the sweater-clad man she had first met as she was from Cinderella.

For a long moment hazel eyes stared into grey ones, but finally it was the man who spoke. There was none of the well-remembered humour in his voice; instead it was polite and toneless, as devoid of expression as the craggy face.

"Good evening, Miss Rosten. So we meet at last."

"Come now, Barnaby," she said lightly, "don't pretend you don't know me." Mentally applauding her control, she moved over to him and held out her hands. "Aren't you even a little bit surprised to find out who I am?"

"Do you need me to tell you that?" he half smiled. "Yes, I suppose you do. All women like to savour their triumph. And tonight must be very triumphant."

"What makes you say that?" she asked thickly.

"The fact that you kept your identity such a secret." He glanced away from her to George Martin. "I take it you know the story, sir?"

The older man nodded. "I played a leading part in it myself."

This time Barnaby showed his puzzlement. "I'm afraid I don't understand."

"I'm Nicola's godfather and she's always called me Marty."

For several seconds Barnaby remained motionless. Then he turned to face Nicola, an odd look in his eyes as he accepted a glass of champagne from her.

"I hope you've also provided a large packet of indigestion tablets," he said.

"What for?"

"If you're planning to make me eat all my words . . ."

Nicola turned away, but not before she saw the sly grin on her godfather's face.

"I've no intention of making you do anything like that," she said coldly. "But just so that we can clear the air I'd like you to know that I never planned any pretence when Mrs. Thomas brought me to the hostel. It happened by accident; by your own attitude. You called me Cinderella, remember?"

"You were dressed in rags."

"I'd run away from a fancy dress party. I was looking for a taxi when Mrs. Thomas knocked me down. The rest you know."

"You're an excellent actress," he said quietly.

"Most women are. And I had an excellent supporting cast Yourself, for example."

His shoulders lifted in a disclaiming gesture, then he picked up the briefcase which he had put on an armchair when he had come in. "Would you like to look at the papers now or after dinner?"

"What papers?"

"Giving details about the hostels. There's a list of all monies expended, the staff engaged, the experiments we're setting up and the –"

"Spare me the details."

"It's what I'm here for. I understood our monthly dinners were to keep you informed about what was happening."

"In a casual way," she drawled. "Reading columns of figures will bore me to death."

He flushed but closed the case, and George Martin came into the conversation, leaving Nicola to sip her champagne and look at Barnaby undisturbed by the fear that he might suddenly turn and look at her. Seeing him again she knew all too clearly that she was as much in love with him as ever – more so, in fact, because she was now seeing another side to his character: that of urbane guest perfectly at home in what could have been an embarrassingly difficult situation. How many other facets did he have to his character, she wondered bitterly, and would he always be able to surprise her as he had surprised her tonight, by accepting the discovery of her identity with barely a lift of his eyebrows?

He leaned forward to illustrate a point to her godfather, and the light from a lamp on a nearby table caught the top of his head, making his hair glow red and reminding her of the first time they had met. But tonight he looked thinner and older, though perhaps it was because of his dark suit. Yet as he turned again she saw a faint speckle of grey in the hair that grew on his temples, and such a strong feeling of tenderness surged up in her that she started to tremble.

Unable to bear his proximity, she stood up. Both men turned to her at once, but before she could speak the butler came in to announce dinner, and feeling she had been saved by the bell she led the way into the dining-room.

No effort had been spared to make the meal a sumptuous one. Beginning with caviar, it ended with Crêpes Suzette, with Lobster Newburg as the entrée. It was a lavish menu that drew a silent look of surprise from George Martin, and the comment that he might be in need of some indigestion tablets himself.

"We don't usually dine so elaborately," he said to Barnaby as the sweet was cleared away and cheese placed before them.

"I think it was laid on in my honour," Barnaby replied gravely, and raised his glass in Nicola's direction. "I appreciate the effort, Nicky."

It was the first time he had called her by this name since he had arrived, and she set her fork down hastily.

"It's no effort to give an order," she replied.

"Far less effort than making mincemeat."

For a split second she did not know what he meant, then as memory returned so did colour to her face.

"That was the easiest part of my act," her voice was high and shaky. "Much better than all that dreadful ironing and washing-up."

"You did extremely well at both jobs. When the revolution comes you need never be out of work!"

George Martin choked on his wine and Barnaby grinned. "That was a joke, sir."

"So I should hope!"

"Barnaby's full of jokes," Nicola replied, "and full of pretences. Which reminds me, how's Joanna?"

"Very well. She's going to feel a fool when she finds out who you are."

Nicola was surprised at the easy way he spoke of his fiancée, but then realised this was typically Barnaby. He was so sure he was right in everything he did that it was impossible to embarrass him by making him feel he was wrong.

"You must bring her here next time you come to dinner," she said brightly.

"That might not be such a good idea."

Again his bluntness startled her, and pushing back her chair she suggested they had coffee in the drawing-room.

As they crossed the hall the telephone rang and automatically she reached out to take it before the butler could come hurrying through the green baize door. It was Jeffrey to find out if there was any possibility of seeing her when the dinner party was over. Aware of Barnaby close at hand, her voice bubbled with delight as she spoke, her conversation punctuated with "darlings" before she finally put down the receiver.

"It was Jeffrey," she explained. "I should really have asked him here tonight too. If it hadn't been for him there wouldn't be any Rosten Homes. I was running away from him the night I ended up at your hostel," she explained, leading the way into the drawing-room.

"The ex-fiancé," Barnaby said beside her.

"I'm not sure about 'ex'," she replied *sotto voce.*

"Does that mean you're engaged to him again?"

With an enormous effort of willpower she forced herself to look directly into Barnaby's eyes. They were as quizzical and gentle as she had remembered, though with fine lines around them that she had not seen before.

"I never really broke the engagement."

"I see."

"You look surprised," she murmured.

"Not surprised; disappointed perhaps."

"Why?"

They were speaking quietly, two people in an oasis of emotion, forming an island together that no one else could intrude on. "I had hoped that the weeks you'd spent at the hostel had

168

taught you something about people . . . something about your-self too."

"Why should you disapprove of Jeffrey?" she persisted. "He's years younger than Marty!"

Barnaby caught his breath and for the first time she knew she had got beneath his guard. "You were so bright and brittle when you were talking to him just now," he said roughly, "that you sounded more like a girl putting on an act than a girl in love."

"I told you I act all the time."

"Why? I can understand Nicky Rose being unsure herself, but not Nicola Rosten."

"Money doesn't always bring confidence," she retorted. "We can't all be as sure of ourselves as Joanna."

"Not many people have had Joanna's settled life," he re-plied easily. "She comes from a happy home and a loving background."

"And a loving future." The words were out before Nicola could stop them.

"She deserves it." His wide mouth curved into a slight smile. "I know you two didn't like each other, but she's a nice person when you get to know her."

"I leave that to you. You mustn't forget to ask me to the wedding."

"What wedding?"

She hesitated, her mouth so dry that she had to moisten her lips before she could speak. "Are you already married, then? If I'd known I'd have asked Joanna here with you."

"I'm not married to Joanna yet."

"I didn't think you believed in long engagements."

"I don't." He reached for his briefcase and took out some papers. "But I won't forget to invite you to the wedding."

"Good," she said brightly, and then flung out her hands.

169

"But put those papers away. I don't want to talk about the hostels. I'm not interested in them."

"Then why did you set up the Trust?"

"It was my way of – of saying thank you for being so – so kind to me when you thought I was down and out."

"It was a very expensive way of saying thank you."

"Nothing's expensive to me," she said bleakly. "Money's the one thing I can afford."

In silence Barnaby put away the papers. "Then you don't want to know how the hostels are doing?"

"I'm sure they're all doing wonderfully," she said with a smile. "You must be helping lots of poor unhappy people."

"Lots of rich unhappy people need helping too."

"If you're suggesting *I'm* unhappy –" she said angrily.

"Aren't you? You're thin as a rake and –"

"It's fashionable to be *slender*. I don't need to fill up on bread and potatoes," she added thinly. "I can afford meat."

He grinned. "Quick-tongued as ever. It's good to see you."

"Even though I made a fool of you?" she asked.

"It was worth being made a fool of. After all, it got me the hostels. It was a marvellous thing to do, Nicky. I'm very grateful."

"I don't want your gratitude."

"What *do* you want?"

"Nothing." She turned away from him. "It was a mistake seeing you tonight. I don't think we'll continue with the monthly meetings."

"Are you bored so easily?"

She swung back to face him and saw his expression was sober. "Not bored, Barnaby. Just realising I don't have the same interests as you. I thought I'd go on being interested in your work, but . . . Well, I'm not."

"In that case I'll go." He still looked sober. "I'm sorry you feel this way about the hostels. I hoped they would relieve your boredom."

"I've too many things to do to be bored," she said lightly.

"Worthwhile things?"

"I leave *that* to do-gooders like yourself and Joanna."

"Fair enough. Then I won't take up any more of your time. I'll be in touch with the Trustees, of course. And if you ever wish for a first-hand report . . ."

"I won't."

His eyes narrowed, but he made no comment as he turned and looked at George Martin. "I hope you'll forgive me for leaving so early, but I've a clinic in the morning."

"I thought you'd given up hospital work?" Nicola could not prevent herself asking.

"Only till I'd organised the hostels. But being at a hospital keeps me on my toes."

"It'll put you in an early grave too. You work too hard."

"No one dies from overwork – only boredom!" He held out his hand. "Goodbye, Nicky. I wish you well. And thanks again – not just from me, but from everyone you'll be helping."

Their fingers met, and though she kept her expression careless, his touch sent an electric current throbbing through her veins, making her conscious of every part of her body, and every part of his. Barnaby, she cried silently . . . Barnaby . . . But aloud, all she said was a cool, "Goodnight."

Only when the sound of his car could no longer be heard in the quiet square did she move from the motionless position she had held in the centre of the room and fling herself on the settee in a paroxysm of weeping. For a long while there was no other sound, but finally the sobbing ceased and she sat up and wiped her eyes.

"You were right, Marty," she gulped. "I should never have asked him here."

"You had to ask him once," her godfather replied. "You're the sort of girl who only learns by her own mistakes."

"It certainly was a mistake. He's so confident," she whispered. "He takes everything in his stride. When he came here tonight and saw me he didn't even show surprise."

"You put on a pretty good act yourself."

"I know," she sighed. "But *he* wasn't acting. He really didn't care." Once more the tears flowed and her godfather sat down beside her and drew her into his arms.

"Forget him, Nicky. You'll never find happiness until you do."

"I'll never find happiness either way." She lifted her head. "But I won't see him any more. There's no point. When you see him again, tell him he can have as much money as he wants and that I wish him the best of luck."

"Is that all?"

"He doesn't need anything more from me," Nicola replied. "He never has."

CHAPTER THIRTEEN

Seeing Barnaby again awakened all Nicola's longing for him, and in an effort to banish him from her thoughts she once more started to lead a hectic social life.

"You'll make yourself ill if you go on like this," George Martin remonstrated one morning as he came in to see her with some contracts that needed her signature. "You look as if you haven't been to bed for a week."

"A good guess, Marty," she responded. "What's the point of going to bed if I can't sleep? At least if I'm with other people I don't think."

"Don't you? You look as if you're doing nothing else. You're haunted, Nicola. Haunted by a man who doesn't want you!"

The cruelty of the jibe was like acid on a raw wound, and the unexpectedness of having it flung at her by Marty was her undoing.

"How can you be so hurtful?" she cried, and burst into tears.

It was the first time she had cried since the night Barnaby had come to see her, but this time the tears were for herself alone, for the lonely seeker of companionship, the frustrated and bored girl searching desperately for love. But the harder one searched the more difficult was the finding. This was something she was beginning to find out. Barnaby was right. Happiness came in its own time. It could not be plucked from the tree of life like a ripe fruit.

"I'm sorry, Nicola." Her godfather came to sit beside her. "I didn't mean to be cruel. But I can't stand by and watch you

173

destroy yourself — any more than I was prepared to have you destroy Grayson."

"He's indestructible," she sobbed. "He believes in the Divine Right of Barnaby!"

"Then accept the fact and forget him. He's in love with someone else and he doesn't want *you*."

"I've told myself that a million times."

"Then say it a million times more! One day it will start to take effect."

"When I'm old and grey."

"Long before then," Marty assured her. "Perhaps if you married Jeffrey . . ."

"I thought you didn't like him?"

"I don't. But it would be better for you to be Jeffrey's wife than widow to a shadow!"

Nicola remembered this when Jeffrey called for her later that evening. By a quirk of fate they were going to a party at Deborah's, and sitting beside him as they drove towards Chelsea she had the strange feeling that she was turning back the clock. If only she could! She clasped her hands in her lap and prayed for the ability to close her mind and her heart to the past.

But Jeffrey's hands, coming down on her hers, brought her hurriedly back to the present. "What's going to happen to us?" he whispered. "I'm crazy about you. How much longer are you going to keep me waiting?"

"I'll let you know in a few days," she murmured, and was relieved when the car stopped outside the tall, brightly lit house in the imposing street.

"Why not now?" he persisted.

"Because we're going to Deborah's party — and you remember what happened the last time we were there."

He caught his breath. "I was drunk then. I told you so. For

heaven's sake, don't keep threatening me with that!"

"I'm not threatening you. I'm just suggesting it's better not to talk about our future until I'm sure I've forgotten the past."

"I could make you forget the past if you'd let me," he said, and purposefully drew her against him.

"No!" she cried, and tried in vain to pull free of him.

But he would not let her go and, deciding that it was as good a time as any to test her reaction to him, she remained quiescent in his arms. But his touch held no magic, nor his lips the power to arouse her, and no matter how hard she tried she could not force reality to blur. It remained crystal clear, each action and sound sharp and magnified: the warmth of his breath on her cheek, the hardness of his arms around her body and the dampness of his forehead as he rested it against hers.

Caught up in his own emotion, he did not recognise that she was devoid of any, and when he finally set her free it was with a contented sound. "You see?" he said. "You do still love me."

Deciding it was less hurtful to pretend, she let her hand rest in his as they entered the crowded marquee which had been set up on the lawn at the back of the house.

It was an excellent party, not too crowded and with a swinging band and a lavish amount of food and drink. Yet though she tried to lose herself in the gaiety, Nicola felt as if she was in a state of suspension, hovering high in the air and looking down upon the body that was hers, watching it as it gyrated on the dance floor or drank champagne.

Jeffrey did not leave her side, determined to prove the truth of what he had said a few hours earlier. But his constant attendance became increasingly difficult for her to bear, and by eleven o'clock she knew she could not face any more of it.

175

She could never marry Jeffrey. The certainty of the knowledge was beyond doubt. There was no need to reconsider it or discuss it with Marty. All at once she saw the path ahead of her, the long lonely route she would never be able to share with another person for many years to come. Perhaps one day she would forget Barnaby sufficiently to consider marrying someone else, but to try and do so now would be courting disaster. There was no point pretending that filling her days with social trivia was helping her to forget the past. Indeed, since she could not forget it she might as well learn to live with it.

Barnaby was right when he said the only way to combat boredom was with work. And this did not mean writing cheques for charity but doing the act of charity oneself.

Unable to bear the noise and heat, she slipped out of the marquee and wandered in the garden. Perhaps she would form another Trust and administer it herself. She did not have the qualification to do the work Joanna was doing, but Barnaby had once told her she had an empathy for the girls at the hostel, and perhaps this could replace the more usual academic degrees.

If she did not love Barnaby so much she would have asked him to let her work in one of his hostels, but even though he might only visit it rarely, it would still be too painful to be connected with him. No, whatever she did, she must stay out of his life.

Beyond the garden wall she heard the intermittent hum of traffic as it rumbled along the embankment, and finding herself by a side door she impulsively unlocked it and stepped outside. She was in a narrow alley that ran behind the houses, and she walked swiftly down it till she reached the main road. Behind her she could still hear the blaring of the orchestra, and several cars laden with people were still turning into the

176

street and stopping outside the brightly lit façade of the house she had just left. It was going to be more crowded there than ever; she could not face the prospect of going back. Jeffrey would be furious when he discovered she had gone, but she did not care.

Slowly she walked along the Embankment. The night was warm and still, the dark sky punctuated by glittering stars like a black velvet eiderdown inlaid with diamonds. The glitter was reflected in the still waters of the river, where not even a ripple stirred the jet surface. In the distance, traffic still streamed over Chelsea Bridge, and she rested her elbows on the parapet and looked out over the river, letting her thoughts drift idly back and forth like one of the boats moored on the other side of the bank.

Footsteps sounded behind her and then stopped. Resolutely she refused to acknowledge them and the footsteps came closer.

"Anything wrong, miss?" a deep voice enquired.

Turning, she saw a young policeman. "Everything's fine, officer," she said, relieved. "Why do you ask?"

As though reassured by her svelte appearance, he half smiled. "Water sometimes has a melancholy effect on people. I wanted to make sure you weren't contemplating jumping in."

"I'm not the type to take that way out."

"It's not always a question of type, miss. You'd be surprised at the unlikely ones who do it. Not destitute people either — but youngsters who you'd think had everything to live for."

An old man shuffled by, a bundle of newspapers in his hands.

"Carrying his blankets with him," the policeman murmured, and glancing at a bench close at hand.

Nicola went to move further along, but the policeman held up a restraining hand. "No need for that. We don't let them

177

doss down here, anyway."

"Where can they sleep if they've got no money?"

He did not answer and she turned back to look at the water again, remembering a night when this pavement had been blanketed by fog and she had been running along it searching for a taxi – as she was now searching for a mode of life.

"There's a hostel near here," she said slowly, "that takes care of young people who've nowhere to go."

"That would be Dr. Grayson's place."

She swung round to look at the policeman again. "You know it?"

"Most of us around here do. He's helped us to settle quite a lot of youngsters who'd otherwise have given us trouble."

"Do you know him – Dr. Grayson?"

"Not personally, miss, but very well by sight. Up till a few months ago he used to wander along here every evening. Made a regular habit of it, he did, walking up and down this stretch of the Embankment from ten at night till two or three in the morning."

It was unusual behaviour for Barnaby, and curiosity impelled her next remark. "He couldn't have been searching for inmates," she said drily. "He hardly had room enough for those who were already there."

"He wasn't looking for *new* ones," the policeman replied, "but for someone who'd been there and run away. All the officers at the station knew about it, but we never got the whole story. Seems one of the girls ran off and Dr. Grayson was trying to find her. Someone had originally discovered her wandering along the Embankment and brought her to the hostel, and he was hoping she'd repeat the pattern and come back here again."

Nicola absorbed the words slowly, afraid she might make

178

the wrong sense out of them. "Did you say he was searching for a girl?"

"That's right — for near on two months. He questioned every policeman on the beat, asked every tramp he found sleeping on the benches — nearly came to blows with some of them. They thought he was demented, waking them up to ask if they'd seen a young girl with long dark hair. Then he suddenly stopped looking. I don't know if he found her or just gave up the search."

"He found her," Nicola said evenly. "I assure you of that."

The policeman looked at her oddly. "I wouldn't stay here too long if I were you, miss. Have you got your car parked handy?"

"I've just escaped from a party." She pointed to the street behind her and the gleaming cars parked nose to tail along both kerbs. "Don't worry about me, officer, I'll be going back there in a couple of moments. I only came out for some peace and quiet."

Reassured, the policeman went on his way, and Nicola leaned against the parapet once more and mulled over what she had just discovered. She could not make any sense of it. There was no doubt Barnaby had been searching for her. But why? Even now she could remember the bitter words he had flung at her when he had discovered that Marty had paid for the book she had given to him, and the fury on his face as he had refused to listen to her explanation. Indeed, the willingness with which he had believed ill of her had sent her from the hostel. Not that she could have stayed there anyway once she had learned of his engagement to Joanna.

Still deep in thought, she walked along the pavement. Night after night for two months Barnaby had tramped these streets in search of her, questioning everyone he met in the hope of finding where she was. What would he have done if he had found her? Apologised for losing his temper and then taken her back to the hostel to try and reform her all over again? She waited for her anger to rise at the thought, but the only emotion that stirred was one of sadness. By coming to look for her he had displayed the compassion that was the essence of his character, a compassion that enabled him to understand it was not always easy to change the pattern of one's life, as he believed she had not found it easy to leave her Marty.

Yet how furious he had been when he had learned she had accepted money from Marty to buy the book of paintings. How furious to think she might leave the hostel and return to a life he thought unworthy of her.

"Get out," he had said. "I never want to see you again."

But his subsequent actions showed her how much he had regretted those words. For more than two months he had searched the dark streets for her; questioned policemen and tramps in an effort to learn her whereabouts. It bespoke a diligence far beyond the call of duty, beyond even his compassionate nature. Yet he had done so, and might have gone on doing it had he not finally discovered that Nicky Rose had never existed at all. In direct contrast to Cinderella who had disappeared from a palace to return to a hovel, Barnaby's Cinderella had returned to wealth and luxury.

She drew a shuddering breath and clasped her hands around her. Her silk dress was not sufficient to ward off the chill breeze blowing in from the Thames, and she looked along the road in search of a taxi. Fancifully she wondered if a little car would come chugging round the corner to knock her down and take her into the past again. But what was done could not be undone, and what was undone could never be put together again.

A young couple strolled by, arm-in-arm, followed by an old man who sidled up to her and held out his hand. She found a fifty-pence piece in her bag and gave it to him, then moved away as he showed signs of talking. There was no taxi in sight and she crossed the mainroad and hurried down a side street. It took her a moment before she realised that the hostel stood some twenty yards ahead of her. She came to a sharp stop, her long skirts swaying round her. She wanted to go nearer, yet fear held her back, and blindly she turned towards the Embankment again. But she could not move; though her mind urged her forward, her limbs refused to obey. In a daze she stumbled towards the house.

It loomed up tall and grey. Light shone dimly through curtained windows und a brighter glow came through the fanlight above the door. Was it still kept open, she wondered, so that anyone could come in for shelter? She went up the path. Was Barnaby here tonight or was he in Birmingham or Manchester, or one of the ten different places which her money had made possible? Yet the money she had given him was not enough. She had to give him her apology too. Had to admit she had misjudged him. He had not cruelly cast her out when he had discovered she had let him down. He had come after her the moment he had discovered she had gone, and had continued to search for her night after night. For this alone she owed him an apology.

Tentatively she put her hand on the door knob; it turned noiselessly and she opened the door and stepped into the hall. Everything was the same, yet not the same. The familiar orange-covered lampshade that inadequately covered the bright bulb suspended from the ceiling was still the same, as was the linoleum-covered floor and biscuit-beige walls. But the paint had been renewed and a large radiator, also new, stood like a sentinel against one wall. No sound could be heard and she glanced at her wristwatch. One o'clock. Most of the people would be asleep. She went into the common room. It was in darkness and she turned back to the hall. As she did so someone came round the stair-well, a slim dark-haired girl with a calm, untroubled face – Joanna.

Nicola moistened her lips and wished with all her heart she had not given way to the impulse to come here. But it was too late for regret and she stood her ground and waited, gaining strength from the knowledge that she could at least meet Joanna on equal terms.

Joanna came nearer, a flush in her cheeks, her eyes bright and hard. "Miss Rosten! I – we weren't expecting you. Barnaby never said you were coming here."

"He doesn't know. I was at a party a few streets away and I –" Nicola shrugged. "I was passing by and thought I'd see if things had changed."

"Everything's the same. We've put in central heating, of course, but I'm sure you know about that."

"I don't."

"Ah, yes. Barnaby said you weren't interested any more."

"What's he doing now?"

"Getting ready to go to the States. He's been invited there for a month's lecture tour. The Ford Foundation are interested in doing what you've done here."

"You mean I might have set the pattern for something?" Nicola asked.

Joanna nodded. "We're all very grateful. I know our gratitude doesn't mean much to you, but –"

"I don't want yours!"

Joanna flushed. "I suppose you're still angry with me."

"Why should I be?" Nicola began, and then stopped, realising that to pretend would not fool Joanna. "I was angry at the time," she conceded, "but it isn't important now."

"Even so, I'm glad you didn't let the things I said stop you from setting up the Trust. Barnaby's so grateful –"

"He's already told me." Nicola moved to the front door and

then stopped. She was so near Barnaby she could not leave without seeing him. Perhaps if she apologised to him for the spirit in which she had set up the Trust — a desire to triumph over him which had proved to be no triumph at all — she would then be able to find a genuine peace of mind. How right Marty had been when he had said that to hurt someone else only made you hurt yourself. "I'd like to see Barnaby," she said aloud.

"He's asleep."

"I thought you said he was packing."

"I didn't mean it literally. He went to his room about half an hour ago and I'd rather not disturb him. He's had a long day at the hospital."

Nicola knew Joanna did not want her to see Barnaby, and though in other circumstances the knowledge would have added to her bitterness, now it only saddened her. Didn't Joanna know she had nothing to fear any more? Barnaby had made his choice and she had won.

"I'll tell Barnaby you were here," Joanna said. "If you wish him to contact you when he gets back from America . . ."

"There's no need," Nicola sighed. "It was silly of me to call so late."

"I suppose time isn't important to you."

"It can't mean much to you, either," Nicola said. "You never used to stay so late."

"I stay here most nights now."

Joanna glanced behind her in the direction of Barnaby's room, and jealousy swept through Nicola like a forest fire in a ten-force gale. It left her shaken and trembling. No matter that logic told her that Barnaby never had been, and never would be, hers, the knowledge that he was sharing his life with Joanna — holding her and kissing her — was more than she could bear. Blindly she went to the door.

"Barnaby will be sorry to have missed seeing you," Joanna said behind her, "but I'm sure you understand."

Still unable to speak, Nicola opened the door. The night formed a dark frame around her pink chiffon dress, outlining the graceful curve of her shoulders and the proud tilt of her head.

The man coming round the side of the stairs stopped sharply as though he had seen a mirage, then hurried forward. "Nicola! What are you doing here?"

Nicola felt the blood drain from her head. She stared at Barnaby without knowing what to say, yet wondering why he was still in slacks and sweater when Joanna had said he was in bed.

"What are you doing here?" he repeated.

"I was just going." To her own ears her voice sounded inaudible, but he seemed to hear her, for his brows rose.

"Nobody told me you'd arrived."

"I thought you were asleep," Joanna put in.

"You should have come to find out."

"I didn't want to disturb you."

"Nicky's entitled to disturb us."

"I'll come back another time," Nicola said. "I only – only came in on an impulse."

She went to step through the doorway and found him by her side. "Where's your car?"

"I haven't got one. I was at a party with Jeffrey and –"

"Not the same house where you were the night you first came here?"

Nicola nodded and was surprised to see the colour seep from Barnaby's face, leaving it with a greyish tinge that made his hair more richly brown by contrast.

"There'd be no mistaking you for Cinderella tonight," he said huskily. "But where's your Prince Charming?"

"I left him at the party. I had a headache and I – I decided to leave early."

"By yourself?"

"There was no reason to spoil his fun."

Barnaby's jaw clenched. "I'll drive you home."

"There's no need. I'll take a taxi."

"I wouldn't dream of letting you."

"Perhaps Miss Rosten prefers to go home alone, Barnaby." Joanna came to stand beside him, her hand lightly touching his arm.

"Maybe she does, but I've no intention of letting her."

"You're making a fuss about nothing." Nicola turned in a swirl of pink chiffon. "And Joanna's right. I do prefer to go home alone."

"Then I'll call you a radio cab," Barnaby said. "It's ridiculous for you to walk along the street like that." He looked at Joanna. "Would you call one for me?"

Watching Barnaby and Joanna, Nicola had the strange feeling that Joanna was going to refuse. Twin flags of red burned in her cheeks and grew brighter still as she swung on her heel and disappeared into the office.

As she did so, Barnaby went over to the sitting room and opened the door. "We might as well wait in here. It's more comfortable."

Silently she followed him, resolutely keeping her head averted from him. She heard him close the door but did not hear any footsteps, and when she glanced round she saw that he was leaning against it, his arms crossed over his chest. No man had a right to look so handsome and uncaring, nor exude such virility at this hour of the night.

"Why *did* you come here, Nicky?" His voice was deep and low.

185

"I told you. I was – I was on my way home and – it was an impulse. You know I do things on the spur of the moment."

"So you said when we last met." His words reminded her of the reason that had brought her here, a reason which no longer seemed easy to explain when he was towering in front of her. Yet she had to explain. Until she did, she would be haunted by it.

"You're right," she said stiffly. "It wasn't impulse that made me come here. I wanted to – to apologise for the things I said when we last met."

"You said so many."

"Don't tease me," she said sharply.

"I find it easier to tease you than to take what you say seriously." His voice had a curious tremor in it. "I don't know how *you* deal with emotion, Nicky, but I find it less difficult if I'm being funny."

She tried to work out what he meant, but her awareness of him made it difficult for her to think clearly, and with the desire to run into his arms growing stronger and stronger she put more of the room between them.

"When I formed the Trust," she said, keeping her gaze fixed on the wall, "I did it for the wrong reasons. I wanted to humiliate you. To make you report to me every month."

"To humiliate me?" he said, puzzled.

"Yes. You'd – you'd hurt me. I realise now that I'd mis-judged you. You couldn't hurt anyone," she whispered. "You're too kind."

"You're always exaggerating," he said. "That's one habit you haven't got rid of!"

"And you were right about me," she went on, ignoring his comment. "It isn't satisfying just to sign cheques and let other people do the work. I need to do something more positive – more active. I won't interfere with – with what you're doing,

186

but I'm sure there are lots of other – other equally worthwhile causes that need me – my money and my help."

"Hundreds," he agreed gravely.

Tears stung her eyes. "You're still being sarcastic, aren't you? Why are you trying to make me dislike you?"

"I didn't think I needed to try."

She drew a deep breath, forcing herself not to lose her control. If only she *could* hate him, how much easier her life would be.

"I hear you're leaving for the States tomorrow." The words came out of her unprimed, surprising her, as they seemed to do him.

"Who told you?"

"Joanna."

"You must have misunderstood her. I'm not going for a couple of weeks yet." He moved from the door and perched on the arm of the settee.

Nervously Nicola backed away, wondering how much longer she would have to wait for a taxi. "I'm surprised you aren't getting married before you go."

He looked up sharply. "Why should I?"

"Then your trip could be a honeymoon."

Abruptly he stood up and she saw the unexpectedly hard set of his chin. "You seem very anxious to get me married, Nicky," his voice was like ice. "Perhaps you can tell me *whom* I should marry?"

"Do I need to?"

"My God, you're a cool one!" He strode over and caught her shoulders with a viciousness he had never shown before. "Don't rely on your exalted position to protect you all the time! A man can take so much and no more." He flung her away from him and she staggered against the table.

"Wh-what's wrong?" she stammered. "Why are you so

187

angry? I thought that – that as you're going to the States – you'd have taken Joanna with you."

His head straightened, and the colour which he had lost earlier returned to his face, but more intensified, as though he were flushed with excitement.

"Why should I marry Joanna?" he asked.

"You're engaged to her."

"I see."

Again Barnaby crossed his hands over his chest, but this time Nicola felt he did so because he was afraid to keep his hands free. Without knowing why, her heart started to pound and she was glad of the support of the table behind her.

"When did you find out I was engaged to Joanna?" he asked conversationally.

"She told me the night you –" Nicola looked at the floor. "Does it matter?"

"Very much."

She saw his feet on the carpet and knew he had come to stand close to her, though it did not need his trousered leg to tell her this, for she could feel the warmth radiating from him.

"I'm waiting for an answer," he said quietly. "When did Joanna tell you I was engaged to her?"

"The night of your birthday."

She heard him expel his breath, but still refused to lift her head.

"Is that why you ran away, Nicky?"

Still she kept her head down. "Certainly not! You told me to go. 'Get out! I never want to see you again.' Those were the words you used."

"You know why I said them. Damn it, you *must* know!"

He pulled her into his arms again, the gesture forcing her head up so that she stared into his face. What she saw there was too overwhelming to believe and she could not speak.

"You know why I told you to go," he reiterated. "Because I believed Marty was your lover and I could have murdered him. I wanted to marry you and I was beginning to believe I could when I – when Joanna made me think I'd been wasting my time."

"You wanted to marry me?" Nicola echoed. "But you never hinted – never . . . I tried so hard to make you admit –"

"I was afraid to admit it. I felt you'd come to the hostel because you wanted a shelter and I was furious with myself because I wanted it to mean much more to you than that. I wanted it to become your life – *our life.*"

"You had a funny way of showing it." Unexpectedly she twisted from his grasp. "I threw myself at you, Barnaby, I made it so obvious I loved you."

"I thought you were being grateful."

"Grateful!"

"Not all the time," he conceded. "But certainly in the beginning. After we went to the discothèque I began to hope you weren't seeing me as a father-figure but as a prospective husband. I almost told you how I felt, but I still didn't think I had the right." He moved purposefully towards her. "I'd finally decided to do so when Joanna told me about Marty buying the book for you and – the rest you know."

"I believed her," Nicola gasped. "She spoke with such conviction."

"I'm afraid the wish was father to the thought." His voice was harsh. "I never gave her any reason to think I loved her. You've got to believe me."

"I believe everything you say," she said simply, her heart in her eyes. "I love you, my darling. That's why I came here tonight. If I hadn't seen Joanna when I got here I'd probably have told you so the minute I saw you."

189

"Let's not talk about Joanna," he said grimly. "When I think of what I went through . . . the hours I spent looking for you."

"I know," she murmured. "I found that out tonight."

He gave a deep, contented sigh. "An hour ago I was wondering how I was going to spend the rest of my life without you. And now . . ." His arms wrapped themselves around her, and he touched his lips to her creamy shoulders. "Will you marry me soon?"

"Is the end of the week soon enough?"

"Let's make it three days. We've already wasted too much time." His mouth was a breath away from hers. "Will you mind being a doctor's wife?"

"Not if you don't mind being an heiress's husband!"

"I love your money," he murmured. "It brought us together!"

"Oh, Barnaby," Nicola said tremulously. "You make everything so sane and logical. I'll never let you escape me now."

"Who's trying?" he asked, and put his lips on hers. "We belong together," he said huskily. "Let me show you."

Why the smile?

... because she has just received her **Free Harlequin Romance Catalogue!**

... and now she has a complete listing of the many, many Harlequin Romances still available.

... and now she can pick out titles by her favorite authors or fill in missing numbers for her library.

You too may have a **Free Harlequin Romance Catalogue** (and a smile!), simply by mailing in the coupon below.

Have You Missed Any of These
Harlequin Romances?

All books are 60c. Please use the handy order coupon.

RR